HER DEADLY DECEPTION

BONZAI
MOON

BonzaiMoon Books LLC
Houston, Texas
www.bonzaimoonbooks.com

Editing by Kelly Hartigan of Xterra Web
http://editing.xterraweb.com

$$1$$

"Ms. Edwards." Sione Tuiali'i stared down at her. "How are you?"

Spencer was speechless. The last time she'd seen the resort owner had been days ago, when she'd stormed into his office to get the package Ben had shipped to her.

Mr. Tuiali'i looked even more delicious than she remembered, wearing nothing but a strange sarong with geometric patterns. Her mouth watered as she stared at his muscles, mesmerized. His broad shoulders, pecs, and arms were huge and exquisitely formed beneath the creamy, brown sugar skin, which was decorated with a plethora of what looked to her like tribal markings.

The tattoos formed strange swirls and whorls across his pecs and eight-pack abs, then moved up to his neck and left shoulder, before traveling in loops and twirls down his left arm, past his elbow to his wrist.

"Ms. Edwards?"

Snap the hell out of it, Spencer. There was no reason to lose her cool. He'd been gorgeous when she first met him, and he was still gorgeous. There was no reason to get so worked up over the way he looked. She didn't have time to drool. She needed to lay more groundwork for getting *Step Two* completed.

The "side venture" was days away, and as pissed as Spencer was about having to do it, she realized there was a silver lining in the situation. The banker's box gave her the perfect excuse to see the resort owner. Spencer figured there was no need to let the next few days go to waste, and she'd come up with a plan to start getting close to him. But not too close.

"Mr. Tuiali'i," Spencer started and then stopped, trying to get her thoughts together.

"Sione."

"Huh?"

"You can call me Sione." He leaned against the doorframe of his house.

"Sione." Spencer cleared her throat and then looked to the left, where a riot of purple and pink hibiscus bushes hung over the wooden railing around the porch. "That's an interesting name. I don't think I've ever heard it before I met you."

"It's Tongan," he said. "Means John."

"Sione is how you say John in Tongan," she said. "So, you're Tongan."

"Half," he said. "My father is from Tonga, my mom is from Belize."

Spencer nodded, not sure what to say, trying to remember why she was there.

"What can I help you with?"

Involuntarily, her gaze dropped to his waist and even lower.

"Ms. Edwards?" he prompted.

She lifted her head. There was a trace of a smile on his lips, with just enough mischief to let her know he'd seen the direction of her gaze.

"I don't mean to bother you. The front desk attendant told me you were working at your casita today, and I just needed to ask you ..." Spencer stopped and exhaled, trying to remember the lie she'd come up with, the excuse to see him.

She'd spent all last night coming up with the ruse, going over it again and again, testing it for faults and flaws. She should know her lines by now. There could be no stuttering and stammering. She couldn't arouse his suspicions before she even got started with the scheme.

Clearing her throat, Spencer continued, "It's about that banker's box I received."

With a sigh, Sione said, "Why don't you come in?"

Spencer didn't know whether to be relieved or ashamed. She didn't like the idea of tricking her way into the resort owner's casita, but the goal had been to get invited inside. An invitation into his casita could not be interpreted as a sign of his willingness to let her get close to him. She couldn't take anything for granted. His hospitality didn't mean he was interested.

Parading in front of a man wearing a clingy dress with her boobs spilling out all over the place might entice him. Rae had taught her lots of clichéd seductive techniques, provocative contrivances that usually worked. On old geezers, at least.

Spencer had never tried those tricks on someone like Sione, who was so good-looking that he left her feeling flustered and uneasy. Geriatric fools responded to batting eyelashes, but the resort owner might see right through her deception. He might even get suspicious and think she was up to something.

Sione led her into the kitchen, then walked to a large marble-top island, and leaned against the rounded edge.

"Now, Ms. Edwards, what did you want to tell me about the package you got?"

"Oh, um ..." she started, reluctant to get on with the business of lying to him, wishing she didn't have to.

Staring down at her, he folded his arms across his chest, a move that made his muscles contract. Spencer gazed at him, wondering why he was so damn distracting. She'd seen handsome, well-built men before, and they'd never had this effect on her, leaving her dumbfounded.

She didn't have time to get lost in his hazel eyes. She had to get on with laying more groundwork for *Step Two*, and yet she was hesitant to start her scam. There was no way to know if her plan to get close to him would work, but she had to try.

Spencer exhaled, taking a few steps toward the island, going over her plan, which would accomplish two objectives. It was simple, really. She would tell the resort owner the wrong box had been delivered to her. With a tone of frustration and anger, she would give him a story about opening the box and being shocked to find boxes of Xanax.

Xanax? Xanax!

She would shift the blame to him, declaring the delivery of the wrong box to be another example of his staff's deplorable inability to provide even the most basic customer service. She would hold him responsible and threaten to sue the resort.

Of course, the resort owner would want to make amends. He would probably ask what he could do to come to some kind of rapprochement. And Spencer would tell him she would be willing to come up with an amicable solution to the problem.

Over dinner, perhaps?

No, maybe dinner would be pushing her luck. Drinks? Maybe coffee, or—

"Ms. Edwards?"

Spencer took a quick, deep breath, trying to stay focused on her scam, and said, "The wrong box was delivered to me."

Eyes narrowed, he stared at her and then said, "It was?"

Nodding, she said, "I was expecting training manuals. That box was full of … Xanax."

2

———

San Ignacio, Belize
Belizean Banyan Resort - Owner's Casita

Sione hesitated, staring down at Ms. Edwards and then said, "I know."

"You knew the wrong box had been delivered to me?" She glared at him. "How the hell would you know that? You said you hadn't looked in the box, but that wasn't true. You lied to me, didn't you?"

Confused and suspicious, Sione tried to process what she was saying, not sure what to think. He'd thought she'd been expecting the shipment. But now she was giving him some story about training manuals?

What the hell was she up to, he wondered.

The past few days, Sione had thought a lot about what he'd found inside that banker's box and he hadn't come up with any solid conclusions. He suspected Ms. Edwards might be up to something criminal—or maybe not.

"Are you going to answer me anytime soon?" Ms. Edwards demanded, arms crossed in a way that enhanced her already over-exaggerated cleavage, which he appreciated, though it might have been a bit much so early in the day. "Why didn't you tell me the wrong box had been delivered? Did you think I wouldn't know the difference between training manuals and Xanax?"

"I didn't know the wrong box had been delivered to you." Sione shook his head and then said, "When I said, 'I know,' I meant that I knew there was Xanax in the box because I looked in it. I shouldn't have done that, and I'm sorry."

"Why did you lie and say you hadn't looked inside the box?" Ms. Edwards asked.

Sione stared at her, trying to get his thoughts together, which was proving to be more difficult than it should have been. Ms. Edwards was very distracting, especially wearing a tan-colored dress made of material that hugged her curves in all sorts of suggestive and enticing ways.

Sione cleared his throat and said, "I thought you might feel awkward or embarrassed if you knew that I knew you were taking anti-anxiety medication."

She frowned, but the furrow between her brows didn't distract from her good looks. "You know, Mr. Tuiali'i, I just might have to pop one of those pills because I am feeling very anxious right now, and do you know why? Because my damn manuals are missing!"

"I'll have my secretary track down the delivery driver," he said, though he was still suspicious of her, still not sure she really had been expecting to find training manuals in that bankers box.

"And what if she doesn't find the delivery guy?"

"Marie has lots of contacts," he said. "I'm sure she'll figure out what happened to your box."

"Somebody better find my damn box," she warned. "Those

manuals contain classified information, and if they end up in the wrong hands, I am going to sue this resort for—"

Three chirps, loud and insistent, interrupted her.

She gave him a gaze that was furious, sultry, and a bit too arousing, considering the current situation. Sione grabbed the phone and stared at the screen. His heart pounded and he struggled to suppress the anger welling within him as he stared at the number. Guatemalan country code. His ex-fiancée.

He wasn't surprised she was calling again even though he'd warned her not to. The last time he'd hung up on her, she'd threatened to call him and worry the hell out of him until he agreed to persuade his father not to kill her. She was still trying to make him believe Richard wanted her dead.

Sione knew better than to believe her. And yet, part of him wondered, what if she was telling him the truth. What if Richard had really threatened to kill her?

Three more chirps cut into his thoughts.

They sounded louder, somehow, as relentless and insistent as his ex-fiancée.

"Are you going to answer it?" Ms. Edwards asked.

"It's not someone I'm interested in talking to right now."

"An old girlfriend?"

"Something like that."

"She just can't get over you?"

"No, she's over me," he said. "She just …"

"What?"

"I told her I would help her with something," he said. "But I didn't do it, and she's not going to let me forget that I let her down. She keeps reminding me that I broke my promise to her."

"What were you going to help her with?" Ms. Edwards asked. "What was the promise you broke?"

"Ms. Edwards," he said, anxious to get off the subject, embarrassed that he'd opened up to her about his ex. "I really need to deal with some administrative issues, so—"

"Forget the damn administrative issues. We need to solve this situation with my missing training manuals," she said. "So, I was thinking—"

"I'll talk to the rest of my staff," he said. "They may know something about who delivered the box."

"Are you going to talk to your staff today?"

"I'll get back to you about that," he said.

"When will you get back to me?"

"Soon," he said. "Do you mind seeing yourself out?"

Glaring at him, she pivoted and strutted out of the kitchen.

What was that old saying? *Hate to see you leave, but love to watch you go.* Sione sighed, dragging a hand down his jaw. His ex had him so pissed, he could hardly think straight. It was probably good Ms. Edwards had left. He might have told her he hadn't just opened the banker's box, but he'd also looked *inside* those boxes of Xanax and was aware of their true contents.

If Ms. Edwards was lying about those manuals, then Sione didn't want her to know what he'd discovered before his cousin, David "D.J." Jones could do a bit of investigating. As the owner of a security firm that specialized in criminal investigation, D.J. was the best person to find out why Ms. Edwards was really in Belize. D.J. had been eager to help when Sione had called him and explained the situation. A little too eager, actually.

Sione wondered if his cousin had been anxious to come home because he missed the family or if he was anxious to get away from New York and the problems with his wife. Whatever the reason, Sione would be glad to see D.J. and get his professional assistance and advice.

His cousin would be landing in Belize City today, in the next three or four hours, and would be able to get started with the investigation almost immediately.

3

"You know the whole story," Sione said. "What do you think is going on?" Anxious, Sione stared at D.J., waiting for his cousin's assessment of the situation.

Reclining on one of the lounges in the large outdoor patio behind the owner's casita, David Jones stared at the label on the longneck beer bottle.

D.J. had arrived three hours ago, as the sun was setting. After getting settled in one of the few vacant casitas, he'd joined Sione on the terrace of the owner's casita for a beer and to find out more about the situation with the "Xanax" Sione had found in the box delivered to Spencer Edwards.

It was now almost ten o'clock, and in the past five hours, they hadn't discussed the reason for D.J.'s impromptu trip to Belize from New York. Instead, they'd been catching up, reminiscing about the past. As much as Sione enjoyed their close camaraderie, he knew D.J. was in Belize to find out what the hell Spencer Edwards was up to.

After providing the backstory about Ms. Edwards' arrival and the attack on her life, Sione had given him the details of the situation with the banker's box. D.J. had listened intently, asking a few questions now and then, for clarity, but for the most part, D.J. had let him tell the story with minimal interruption. Now Sione wanted to hear his cousin's speculations, but he wasn't sure what he wanted D.J. to tell him. Did he want his own suspicions proved or discredited?

After his conversation earlier this afternoon with Ms. Edwards, Sione had come to some new conclusions. His deductions had veered into another direction, one he was more inclined to want to believe. A direction he hoped D.J. might share, or maybe at least consider.

But D.J. was the security expert, a private investigator whose military career had involved stints in special forces and several "black ops" assignments. Sione would trust D.J.'s judgment and opinions, even if he might not necessarily agree with them.

"I want to make sure I got the facts," D.J. said. "You picked up one of the boxes of Xanax and it felt too heavy."

Sione said, "So I opened it."

"And inside the box of Xanax," D.J. said, "was money and a passport."

"Two hundred and fifty thousand dollars in one-hundred-dollar bills."

"And you found the same thing in the other boxes," D.J. said. "So, a total of seven hundred fifty thousand dollars and three fake passports."

"Not sure the passports were fake."

"Probably were," D.J. said.

"I made copies of all three passports," Sione said. "I don't remember the names, but the passports were for three women."

"Wait, you mean three different women?" D.J. asked. "These weren't three passports with Spencer Edwards' photo and different names?"

"Ms. Edwards' picture wasn't on any of the passports," Sione said. "None of the women looked anything remotely like her. Two white women and a lady who looked Hispanic."

"The passports were probably stolen," D.J. said. "Spencer Edwards is probably going to remove the photos of the two white women and the Hispanic woman and replace them with photos of herself."

"Not necessarily," Sione said and wasn't surprised when his cousin gave him a dubious look. "We don't really know what's going on with the money and the passports. I don't think we need to jump to a negative conclusion without any facts to support it, that's all."

"You sure that's all?"

Deciding to ignore his cousin's insinuation, Sione said, "I'm not sure she knows that almost a million dollars was hidden in those boxes."

D.J. took another swig from his beer and then asked, "What makes you think that?"

"She came to see me earlier to tell me the wrong box had been delivered to her. I really think she expected training manuals to be in that box. I think she was shocked when she saw the Xanax."

"Maybe," D.J. said and then shrugged. "Or maybe she was trying to throw you off her scent."

When Sione had first opened the boxes of pills and seen those stacks of one-hundred-dollar bills, he'd thought Ms. Edwards was a thief or an extortionist. Maybe she was involved in some kind of white-collar crime. Now he wasn't sure she knew about the money.

And if she really hadn't been expecting the cash, then it was possible the money had been delivered to her by accident, which meant the person who was supposed to have received the money would do whatever was necessary to find out what had happened to it. If that person somehow found out the boxes of Xanax had been mistakenly delivered to Ms. Edwards, she could be in a lot of trouble, which worried him.

"Now, about the Asian dude," D.J. said.

"What about him?" Sione asked and grabbed a beer from the cooler.

"You sure she didn't open the door and invite him inside?" D.J. asked.

Sione frowned. "I caught the son of a bitch trying to hogtie her."

"That doesn't sound like a robbery," D.J. said. "Most burglars follow the path of least resistance. They grab and go. They don't take time to tie up the victim. They don't usually risk robbing a place when the victim is present."

"She might have surprised the guy," Sione reasoned.

"She might be working with him," his cousin said. "Check your security surveillance. Find out if she let him in."

"I did, but he was able to evade the security cameras, and there's no way to tell how he got in. I don't think she's working with the guy, though," Sione said. "I'm not even sure she's running a scam."

D.J. reached for another beer from the small cooler on the ground between their chairs. "The woman had seven hundred fifty thousand dollars and three fake passports delivered to her."

"But we don't know why," Sione pointed out. "We don't know anything for sure. We don't even know if the passports are fake."

"Are you serious?"

"Could be a legitimate reason why she had the money and

passports shipped to her," Sione said, aware of how ridiculous he sounded. "Not necessarily something illegal."

"You hope there's a rational reason," D.J. said. "I'm sure you don't want her to be running a scam."

"Of course, I don't want her to be a con artist," Sione agreed, but he was pissed at D.J.'s pointed, accusing tone and upset that he might have to defend his reasons for simply wanting to give Ms. Edwards the benefit of the doubt. "I don't like the idea of criminals at my resort."

"That's the only reason?" D.J. asked, a bit of amusement beneath the innuendo.

"What other reason would there be?"

D.J. shrugged.

Sione asked, "How do you think the situation with Ms. Edwards should be handled?"

"Simple surveillance," D.J. said. "Starting tomorrow."

"You're just going to spy on her?" Sione asked.

"Works every time," D.J. said, smiling.

"You think you'll be able to find out what she's up to?" Sione asked, not convinced spying would produce the results he needed.

"I'll find out what kind of scam Ms. Edwards has going on," D.J. said. "But when I do, will you be able to accept the truth about her?"

"Yeah," Sione said, but he wasn't sure if he was ready to believe Ms. Edwards was some kind of con artist.

"I guess we'll see," his cousin mumbled, loud enough for him to hear.

"We'll see what?"

"We'll see if you can accept the truth that she's a scam artist."

"You think I won't be able to accept the truth?"

"You had a hard time accepting the truth about—"

"Don't say her name."

"Sorry," D.J. said. "Forgot."

"You'll conjure her up," Sione said, leaning back against the chair, looking up at the expansive, star-filled night sky. "And I've already had enough of her."

"What do you mean?"

"She's been calling me recently," Sione said, then finished the beer, and sat the bottle on the ground.

D.J. frowned at him. "And you've been answering her calls?"

"Well, it's my own damn fault that she's calling," Sione said. "I told her I would help her."

"That's what I don't understand," D.J. said. "Why the hell would you agree to help her after what she did to you?"

Sione hesitated and said, "At the time, I thought it was the right thing to do, but now …"

Now the obligation he'd felt two years ago was long gone. He wasn't sure he could explain what had driven his decisions back then. His motives weren't clear, even to himself. Initially, his ex's desperation had compelled him to help her.

Sione suspected his offer to help had been nothing more than a chance to prove to himself that his uncle's influence had prevailed over the violent dictates of his father's instruction. He couldn't explain that to D.J., or to anyone for that matter, without exposing his past. Revealing the depths of Richard's terrorism was something Sione wasn't willing to do.

His maternal relatives believed Richard was a shady businessman with a talent for circumventing the law when it suited him. As far as Sione was concerned, they would never know anything more. He was never going to tell them the truth about his father. No one would know he'd been raised to be just like Richard.

"The right thing to do is to forget about her," D.J. said. "She wasn't the right woman for you. You need to find somebody who really cares about you. Somebody who means what they say. You don't need somebody who will lie and pretend they want to work things out when they really have moved on and don't want to be in the relationship."

"You speaking from experience?"

D.J. glared at him.

"Sorry," Sione said.

Clearing his throat, D.J. said, "So, what does your ex want you to help her with?"

You have to help me … Richard wants me dead.

"I don't want to get into it right now," Sione said, trying to forget her desperation. "I don't want to think about my ex-fiancée."

4

San Ignacio, Belize

Belizean Banyan Resort - Owner's Casita

"Well, Ms. Edwards had a very interesting day," D.J. said, taking a seat at the island in the kitchen. After opening his laptop, he began typing, fingers flying over the keys.

Anxious to learn what his cousin had found out, Sione grabbed two beers from the refrigerator, opened them and pushed one across the counter toward his cousin. "What did she do?"

"I have a presentation." His cousin opened the beer and took a swig from the bottle. "PowerPoint."

Sione raised his beer in salute. "Impressive."

"I thought you would appreciate it." D.J. turned the laptop at an angle where he could access the keyboard and Sione could see the screen.

A few feet away, standing next to one of the empty chairs, Sione waited for his cousin to get started. He was curious but worried. Was

Ms. Edwards a con artist? Did D.J. have proof of her committing some sort of criminal act? If so, what was he going to do about the situation? Confront Ms. Edwards and tell her to leave the resort?

"So, here we go," D.J. said. "Slide one. Ms. Edwards' day begins early. Around seven o'clock. She leaves the casita."

D.J. had captured her mid-stride, walking down the porch steps. She was wearing shorts and a white shirt beneath a denim jacket and a frown on her face—maybe from frustration, consternation, or concentration. Maybe she wasn't a morning person. Nevertheless, she looked damn good.

"I wonder if she wakes up looking like that," D.J. mused. "Beautiful girl."

Sione shrugged, but he was rattled by Ms. Edwards' good looks, more than he thought he should be.

"Slide two. Ms. Edwards visits the resort gift shop." D.J. tapped the ENTER key and the photo changed. "She bought three beach bags."

"I wonder why three bags?"

"Maybe to put three Xanax boxes in."

Sione stared at the photo, trying to ignore the apprehension he felt. There was a proverbial saying about bad things happening in threes. Had Ms. Edwards bought the beach bags because she needed them to do some bad things? He warned himself to wait until D.J. was finished with the presentation before he jumped to conclusions.

The photo changed to Ms. Edwards leaving the gift shop.

"She went back to the honeymoon casita," D.J. said. "Then maybe fifteen, twenty minutes later, she left again and headed down to the main building, and then ..." D.J. hit ENTER.

On the screen, Ms. Edwards stood in front of the resort. To her outfit, she'd added sunglasses and one of the beach bags she'd bought, the pink one.

"So, about ten minutes later, a tour bus shows up. Angie's Eco-Adventures."

Ms. Edwards got on the bus.

"The Belizean Banyan has its own guided tours," Sione said. "Why would she book with some independent company?"

"Your tours are exclusive for your guests only, right?"

Sione nodded.

"Well …" D.J. trailed off and then said, "Wait. You'll see."

The next photo was the tour bus in the parking lot at Xunantunich.

"So, she went to visit Mayan ruins."

"That's what the next few shots are," D.J. said, reconfiguring the settings to slideshow mode.

Sione kept his eyes on the screen, though he was wary, waiting for some photographic evidence of Ms. Edwards' malfeasance. At the same time, he hoped the photos would turn out to be much ado about nothing, just a pictorial of a lovely woman out for a day of sightseeing.

The photos changed every three seconds. Ms. Edwards walking with the group of tourists. Ms. Edwards listening to the tour guide. Ms. Edwards climbing steps of Xunantunich. Ms. Edwards taking a photo of a couple.

The photos continued, each frame a composition of crumbling, sun-bleached stone structures stacked into pyramidal shapes against the backdrop of lush, verdant rainforest. As he watched the slideshow, Sione realized there wasn't one bad picture of Ms. Edwards. She was stunningly beautiful in each photo.

"She never once took any pictures herself," D.J. remarked. "Who goes to Xunantunich without a camera?"

"Maybe she forgot it."

"Or maybe she didn't go there to sightsee."

"Then why go?" Sione asked, but he knew what his cousin was suggesting.

Whatever Ms. Edwards' scam was, it was about to go down at the ruins.

"Now, the tour is over." D.J. ended the slideshow, went back to manual mode, and hit ENTER. Sione stared at a photo of Ms. Edwards getting back on the large passenger bus.

"An hour later, the bus pulls up in front of the Belizean Banyan," D.J. said, narrating the next set of photos. "Ms. Edwards gets off the bus. And she's missing something."

Sione leaned closer to the laptop, peering at the photo of Ms. Edwards entering the resort. "The pink beach bag," Sione realized. "Where is it? Did she accidentally leave it on the bus?"

"Not quite," D.J. said. "Nothing she does is by accident."

The next photo showed a group of five people getting off the bus at a neighboring resort.

"Take a look at the girl in the sun visor."

"What about her?" Sione asked, focusing on a woman in khaki shorts and a white T-shirt with a yellow visor pulled down low, obscuring her eyes.

"Here's a better picture," D.J. said.

The next photo was the girl in the sun visor by herself, a head-to-waist shot of her walking toward the front entrance of the hotel. On her shoulder was Ms. Edwards' pink beach bag.

The photo was a punch in the gut. A sucker punch. Sione wasn't prepared for the onslaught of disappointment he felt.

He wanted proof that Ms. Edwards was innocent, not guilty. D.J.'s surveillance suggested that Ms. Edwards might be up to something criminal. Possibly. But Sione wasn't ready to commit to a guilty verdict. The photos, while suggestive of guilt, weren't exactly conclusive. There could be several conflicting, competing interpretations of what had actually happened.

"Are you sure that's the same pink bag that Miss Edwards had when she got on the bus?"

D.J. scowled at him. "Did you really just ask that?"

"The photos don't prove that she committed a crime," Sione said. "We don't even know what was in the beach bag. You think it was the money, but you don't know for sure."

"You're right," D.J. conceded. "But I do know something about the girl in the visor."

"What do you know about her?" Sione asked, folding his arms as he stared at his cousin.

"Take a closer look. Recognize her?"

"Should I?"

"Keep looking," D.J. said and then pulled a blue folder from the side pocket of his laptop bag. D.J. took out copies of the passports Sione had discovered in the Xanax boxes. He slid a copy of one of the passports across the granite countertop toward Sione.

Sione stared at the copy of the passport and then at the photo of the girl in the visor, magnified on the screen to two hundred percent. Another hit in the gut, but not as bad as the first one. The disappointment wasn't as sharp either.

"So, the girl in the yellow visor is Anna Rivera," Sione said, glancing at the name on the copy of the passport and back at the laptop screen.

"No, the girl in the yellow visor is Carla Garcia."

"I don't understand."

"I followed the girl in the yellow visor to her hotel room, and then I did a bit of asking around and found out she checked into the hotel as Carla Garcia," D.J. said. "I was able to take a look at the ID she presented to the hotel upon checking—"

"How?"

"Friends," D.J. said, smiling. "You should make them often. They come in handy."

"Go on."

"After I got a look at her ID, I did a quick background check," D.J. said. "Carla Garcia is unemployed at the moment, but six months ago, she was working in Houston at a payday loan business called Kwik Kash."

"What does that matter?"

"Well, Carla Garcia doesn't work there anymore because Kwik Kash burned to the ground," D.J. said. "Suspicious circumstances. Might have been arson. I'm waiting on a call from a contact to get the details. But what I found interesting is that Carla Garcia has a criminal record. A minor theft charge. But still, people with criminal records don't usually get hired to handle large amounts of cash."

People with criminal records. Like his ex-fiancée. Who was still leaving Sione messages, insisting Richard was determined to put her in the dirt because she'd refused to help him steal something from Ben Chang.

Ignoring the thoughts about his ex, Sione said, "Okay, so you're convinced that the beach bag Ms. Edwards *accidentally-on-purpose* left on that bus contained money and a possibly fake passport?"

"I'm convinced that Ms. Edwards delivered money and a fake passport to Carla Garcia," D.J. said.

"But why?" Sione asked, rubbing his jaw. "Who told her to make the delivery?"

D.J. said, "Maybe you should think about calling Jared."

"Why would I call him?" Sione frowned, thinking about his cousin Jared Camareno, a by-the-book San Pedro police department detective.

"Because possession of a fake passport is a crime," D.J. said.

"What if Ms. Edwards doesn't know the passport is fake?"

"You should call the cops."

"And tell them what?"

Frowning, D.J. said, "That Ms. Edwards has committed a crime."

"We don't know that for sure. Ms. Edwards' behavior is suspicious," Sione allowed. "But these photos are not concrete evidence that any kind of crime was committed. Don't forget, we don't know what was in that beach bag she left on the bus."

"Yeah, you're right. We don't. I think there was money and a fake passport in the bag. But maybe it was tubes of lip gloss or granola bars." D.J. shrugged. "So, I'll continue to keep my eyes and ears open. Eventually, she'll slip up and reveal herself to be the liar that I'm sure she is."

5

Numbers swam and floated before Sione's eyes. For the past hour, he'd been trying to review the latest cash flow projections Truman had given him, but he couldn't concentrate, couldn't stop thinking about his ex-fiancée and her crazy allegations. He'd tried to convince himself that her claims were baseless and not worth the time and mental energy he was wasting worrying about them.

But he couldn't.

His ex claimed his father had visited her in prison, and it was time to find out if that was true. Quickly, before he had a chance to talk himself out of it, Sione called her attorney again. When the receptionist answered, he hesitated but then forced himself to ask for Walter Perales.

Minutes later, the attorney was on the line. Heart slamming,

Sione stumbled through the perfunctory, polite greetings as he tried to think of how he would phrase his request.

"Mr. Tuiali'i," Walter Perales said. "I actually had you on my list of people to call about—"

"I already know," Sione cut the attorney off, anxious to get to the nature of a call he really didn't want to make.

"You already know?" Perales sounded confused. "Did the prison notify you?"

"What are you talking about?" Sione asked, confused. "What would the prison notify me about?"

"You said you knew," Perales said. "I just assumed maybe an official from the prison had told you."

"No one from the prison called me about anything," Sione said. "Why would they?"

"Mr. Tuiali'i," Perales said. "I know the two of you were no longer on the best of terms, but ..."

"But, what?" Sione clutched the receiver, his heart slamming.

"She's dead."

"Dead? Did you say ... ? Wait a minute," Sione said, even though he needed more than a minute. "What are you talking about? How could she be dead? I just talked to her a few days ago."

"I was informed of her passing yesterday afternoon," Perales said. "The warden called me. There was a riot, then fighting broke out. It turned into a huge brawl, and several of the prisoners were seriously injured. Along with four other women, she was stabbed."

Sione closed his eyes and tried to breathe, to concentrate, to figure out what he could say to dispute the attorney's story. It couldn't be true. She couldn't be dead.

"I just received a preliminary report from the prison hospital," Perales said. "There will be an autopsy, but what I know so far is that some sort of homemade weapon pierced her lung. She was transported to the infirmary with the other victims. The doctors did surgery, but she died on the operating table."

"That doesn't make any sense."

"Mr. Tuiali'i, I know this is difficult news to hear," Perales said. "Unfortunately, riots and fights among prisoners are not uncommon, which is why I was working so diligently on her case, trying to get her out of—"

"So, she was stabbed by another prisoner?" Sione asked, troubled by the subtle indictment in the attorney's tone, a sly reminder of the promises he hadn't kept to his ex. He couldn't help but wonder if her death was his fault. If he'd believed her and hadn't been so quick to think she was just trying to trick him, would she still be alive?

"Yes, it is my understanding that she was stabbed by a fellow inmate," Perales said. "But please understand that she was not specifically targeted. She was merely in the wrong place at the wrong time."

The wrong place at the wrong time. A ridiculous platitude meant to pacify, Sione guessed. The attorney's trite explanation of the reason for his ex-fiancée's death pissed him off and made him feel even guiltier. Maybe she wouldn't have been in the wrong place at the wrong time if Sione had kept his promise.

"Mr. Tuiali'i, unfortunately, I'm going to have to cut our conversation short," Perales said. "I have a meeting in a few minutes, but I will call you if I get any additional information."

Mumbling a goodbye, Sione replaced the receiver and then sat back in his chair. He took a deep breath and then another one. His ex-fiancée was dead. He didn't know what to think or how he was supposed to feel.

The emotions churning within him were strange and confusing, hard to identify. Impossible to control, the disbelief and shock threatened to devour him. But the guilt was worse. Impossible to ignore, Sione worried it might consume him.

Richard wants me dead.

Had his father arranged for his ex's death in some staged prison fight? More importantly, did he want to know? He should want answers about his ex-fiancée, shouldn't he? He should demand answers. If his father had set things in motion for his ex-fiancée to be killed, then Richard should be arrested, tried for the crime, and then appropriately punished.

Exhaling, Sione dragged a hand down his jaw. He wanted answers, but finding out the truth would require interaction with his father. And that was something he wasn't willing to do.

6

—————

San Ignacio, Belize
Belizean Banyan Resort

After two days of raining as if it might not stop for forty days and forty nights, the sun was out again. It was a lovely afternoon with brilliant white clouds in an expansive blue sky.

Spencer had spent the final rainy hours this morning at the hotel spa, trying to relax as hot stones were placed down the spine of her back. Her mood was too self-defeating to enjoy the circular stimulation of the smooth stones against her skin. Mystical music and heady incense couldn't make her forget, even for a few moments, the favor Ben was forcing her to do.

She couldn't stop kicking herself for deciding to "date" Ben. Maybe she never would. Maybe she shouldn't. Maybe the self-condemnation and self-loathing was necessary, and it would help her escape the doom of repeating the past.

After the massage, Spencer had gone back to her casita, changed into a tiny powder blue string bikini, and made her way to the pool area. It was a nice afternoon. Too damn nice for manipulation and deceit, but what choice did she have? She had to get this damn favor for Ben over and done with so she could move on with her life such as it was, or even could be.

She found an unoccupied chaise lounge beneath an umbrella near the deep end of the pool and stretched out on the soft, downy cushion. Thank God, the sun was out again.

The rain had thrown a wrench into her program. After she'd pitched a fit about a banker's box full of Xanax instead of the confidential training manuals she'd been expecting, the resort owner had promised to question his employees to find out who had delivered the box. Continuing her ruse about the missing manuals, Spencer had decided she would visit the resort owner for an update on the progress of his inquiry.

Unfortunately, the rain had come down in violent torrents, as though Belize was in the throes of an angry monsoon season, and she'd been stuck inside. Weather-related confinement had given her a vicious case of casita-fever. Bored out of her mind, she'd spent most of the forty-eight hours watching old movies on cable, distracting herself with an Audrey Hepburn marathon. When she wasn't watching television, she was on the phone with her sisters, rehashing everything that had happened during her tour to the Mayan ruins. Because of the rain, Spencer hadn't seen the resort owner. Hopefully, today she would run across him or into him. Whatever. She needed to get on with getting close to him. *But not too close.*

Across from her, near the shallow section, dozens of hotel staff scrambled around, setting up tables and festooning the area with decorations suggestive of a luau—Hawaiian print tablecloths, tiki torches, and flowered leis.

Spencer wondered if some newly married couple was having their wedding reception at the resort later tonight. Absently, she started to imagine what sort of wedding reception she might want. If she ever got married, which she probably wouldn't. Wary of the strange, pointless feelings, Spencer slipped an arm into the bag next to her lounge chair and pulled out her cell phone, thinking she might call Rae or Shady.

"Ms. Edwards?"

Heart in her throat, Spencer gasped, dropped the cell phone, and then flipped over on her back. Standing above her, blocking the sun, was Sione Tuiali'i. Spencer sat up on the chaise, breathing deep, immediately embarking on a desperate search for her towel, painfully self-conscious, for some reason, in her tiny baby blue string bikini, which made no damn sense. Hadn't she been hoping he would see her in the bikini, hoping he would respond in a way that would indicate his interest in her, which might help her get close to him?

"Sorry I startled you," he said.

Shaky, Spencer looked up into his beautiful hazel eyes, momentarily unable to speak, acutely aware of a sly swirling between her legs.

Sione bent down, picked something up, and then extended a hand toward her. "Here's your phone."

Spencer snatched the phone from him, irritated by her response to the tall, impossibly muscular resort owner. If she was going to complete *Step Two*, then he needed to be hypnotized by her. She couldn't be scatter-brained and awestruck by him.

"I see you're taking advantage of the nice weather."

"Well, the sun came back out." Spencer shrugged, staring toward the pool, watching the slight ripples caused by the sultry breeze. "So I figured why not."

"We had a weather system stall over the area for a few days," he said. "But it cleared out, thankfully, or I would have had to cancel the event tonight."

"The event?" Spencer glanced over toward the shallow end, where three hotel workers were spreading tablecloths over the tables clustered in front of a wall of tall privacy hedges.

"Retirement party for a bank executive," Sione said.

Spencer nodded, feeling a bit surer of her looks, pulling one knee toward her chest. "So, I'm actually glad to see you."

"What a coincidence," he said and smiled. "I'm glad to see you, too. I've been kind of worried about you."

"Worried about me?"

Sione pulled another lounge chair close to hers and sat on the edge of it. "Because of that asshole who attacked you."

"You don't need to worry about me," she snapped. "I told you, I don't need a hero. I can take care of myself. I always have, and I always will."

A tense, awkward silence followed as Sione stared at her, an odd look in his hazel eyes that Spencer couldn't fathom, and quickly, she looked away. Focusing on her toes, she mentally kicked herself for her aggressive declaration of independence. She was supposed to be getting close to him, not turning him off with her willful self-reliance. She should have played the damsel in distress. Men liked helpless women. They liked to be the hero, rushing in to save some hapless girl from her own self-destructive devices.

"So," Sione cleared his throat. "How are you enjoying the honeymoon casita?"

"It's lovely," she said, thankful for an opportunity to rectify her misstep. "But I wish I was in one of the deluxe casitas."

"Why do you say that?"

"Because," she said. "I'm not on a honeymoon. I'm not even married."

Nodding, he said, "And why is that?"

"Why is what?"

He hesitated and then smiled a little. "Why is there no husband?"

"You think there should be?"

"I'm surprised there isn't," he admitted.

"Why are you surprised?"

"Because you're really beautiful," he said.

Spencer looked at her toes again, not sure she could trust his compliment. She'd been waiting for a solid confirmation of her beauty from him, but she still wasn't sure being beautiful would matter or if she could rely on her good looks to help her get close to him. "Well, believe it or not, being beautiful doesn't guarantee you a boyfriend," she told him. "Or even a friend with benefits."

"So, you're not seeing anyone?"

"Not at the moment."

"Do you date?"

Spencer froze a moment, thinking of the word "date" and her warped definition of what it meant. "Um, no, not anymore."

He gave her a sly smile and then said, "I can't believe nobody's interested."

"No, they're interested," she said. "But not in me. Not really."

"What do you mean?"

"They're not interested in getting to know me," she said and then shrugged. "But what am I saying, I'm acting like I'm worth getting to know, or something, when that couldn't be further from the truth."

"Why don't you think you're worth getting to know?"

"Because there's no point in getting to know me." She looked away and then back at him. "I would only be wasting somebody's time, you know, since I'm not really into all that love and marriage foolishness."

"Love and marriage foolishness?"

"It's not for me." She glanced toward the opposite end of the pool, where the staff was bringing out more chairs for the event. "I'm not going to be finding my soul mate any time soon."

"How do you know?"

She looked at him. "Because I've planned it that way."

"Sometimes plans don't work out the way you think they will," Sione said.

Spencer didn't need him to tell her that. She already knew plans could blow up in your face, like a hand grenade. She'd learned the hard way and had the scars to prove it. "I don't plan on falling in love and getting my heart broken," she said.

He smiled a little. "But what if you do fall in love and end up with a broken heart?"

"I won't because I stay away from love and romance and all that crap," Spencer said. "It never works out, and you just end up wasting your time and effort and devotion on someone who doesn't give a damn about you after all."

"Are you speaking from experience?"

"What?"

"Did you end up wasting your time and effort and devotion on someone who didn't give a damn about you after all?" Sione asked. "Is that why you don't want love and romance?"

She stared at him, thinking about his question, wondering how to answer it. "No, I just …" Flustered, she said, "Love just makes people too emotional, and I don't want to work myself up into an emotional hissing fit for nothing."

"It's hard not to get emotional when you love someone."

"And that's another problem," Spencer said, glancing at him. "This ridiculous way people have of over-emphasizing love. They make it much more important than it really is."

Sione looked at her, and she had the feeling he thought she was crazy, even though the corners of his mouth lifted. "You don't think love is important?"

"It is," she allowed. "But not as much as people think. You can't live on love, you can't pay the mortgage with love, the light company is not going to waive your payment because the two of you love each other with such staggering and exceeding passion."

"Maybe you're afraid," Sione said.

Scoffing, she looked at him. "Afraid of what?"

"Of loving someone with staggering and exceeding passion."

Heart slamming, she looked at him, realizing she had no response, no counter to his observation, no way to prove him wrong. Sione stared at her, a challenge in his hazel gaze, and soon the silence became heavy, uncomfortable. Minutes that felt like weeks passed.

Finally, Spencer said, "Well, um—"

"Mr. Tuiali'i! Mr. Tuiali'i!" One of the hotel staff hurried toward him, a frantic look in her dark eyes. "I hate to bother you, but we need you."

Sighing, Sione told the staffer he was on his way.

"Before you go," Spencer said. "I wanted to ask you for an update about my missing manuals? Did you talk to your employees? Does anyone know who delivered the wrong box to me? Has my box been found?"

"Unfortunately, no, not yet. But my secretary is still working on it," he said, then stood, and stared at her, his eyes moving along her body from her feet and up her legs to her stomach and her breasts, where he paused long enough to cause the swirling between her legs to intensify, and finally, his gaze lifted to her face. "But hopefully we can get the manuals back to you ASAP. Enjoy the sunshine, Ms. Edwards."

As Sione walked away, Spencer let out a sigh of relief, feeling a little better about her ability to complete *Step Two*. Not only had he told her she was beautiful, but his long, lingering gaze gave her a bit more confidence, enough to decide that he might be interested in her.

Maybe getting close to him wouldn't be so difficult, after all. Maybe. Still, just because he'd called her beautiful didn't mean he'd let her get close to him. *Close, but not too close.* Well, she didn't plan to get too close to Sione. She didn't care how good-looking and sexy he was. The resort owner wasn't the kind of guy she would ever give her heart to. He would surely break it into a thousand razor-sharp pieces.

And when he found out what kind of woman she was, how she'd drugged men to steal from them, he would want nothing to do with her. Spencer shook her head. Why the hell was she speculating about giving her heart to Sione? It was never going to happen because she wasn't going to give her heart to a man. Her decision had nothing to do with any lingering "mommy" issues or any fear of loving someone with staggering passion or whatever the hell.

Suddenly a bit irritated by the blue skies and sunshine and annoyed by all the love and romance talk, Spencer decided to pack up and go back to her casita. Standing, she grabbed her beach bag and then turned. The cab driver who'd called her a bitch was standing in front of her, leering as his gaze dropped to her breasts.

"What the hell do you want?" She took a step back, away from his rank smell and damp face.

"Got a message from Mr. Chang for you," he said, swiping a finger across his top lip.

"What kind of message?" she asked, wary.

"It's time for *Part Two* of the side venture."

7

San Ignacio, Belize

Belizean Banyan Resort - Owner's Office

The door opened as Sione was ending a call with a vendor, and when D.J. poked his head into the office, he beckoned for his cousin to come in as he replaced the receiver on the base.

"Got some more information about Kwik Kash," D.J. said, taking a seat. "Remember I told you the place burned to the ground. Fire was suspicious. Well, initially it looked like an insurance scam. You know, the place isn't doing well, so the owner burns it down to collect a check and start over. But then they found a body among the ashes and charred rubble."

"Someone was killed in the fire?"

"Olivia Eastman was the victim's name, and it was theorized that she stole the money from the Kwik Kash safe then torched the place to cover up her dirty deed but ended up trapping herself inside the building in some strange, freakish accident," D.J. said. "But that's just a theory. Seemed reasonable. Eastman also had a record, like Carla Garcia, and she supposedly owed money to some shylock in Jersey, so she might have been desperate."

"And what does this have to do with Ms. Edwards."

"I was hoping to find a connection between Ms. Edwards and Olivia Eastman, but no such luck," D.J. said. "The connection is between Carla Garcia and Olivia Eastman. They worked at Kwik Kash together. Would have been nice to go to Jared with evidence that Ms. Edwards passed money and a fake passport to one of her former co-workers, but ..."

"Listen, I need to talk to you about something," Sione started and then trailed off, not quite sure how to phrase his request.

"What is it?" D.J. asked.

Sione sighed, worried he might lose his nerve and convince himself to forget about asking his cousin for help.

Since he'd learned of his ex-fiancée's death two days ago, Sione had made a few decisions. If Richard had been involved with his ex-fiancée's death, then he had to know. He figured the first thing to do was to find out if she'd been lying about Richard coming to visit her in prison.

Yesterday, Sione had called her lawyer again, but Walter Perales had refused to give him the information. Frustrated, but not surprised by the attorney's reluctance, Sione had eventually thought of D.J. With contacts all over the place, his cousin could possibly get him the information he needed, but he wasn't sure he wanted to get D.J. involved in this mess with Richard and his ex-fiancée. Asking his cousin for help was risky. D.J. would have questions, and Sione didn't want to lie. He didn't want to disclose Richard's possible involvement if he didn't have to. If his ex had lied, as Sione figured she had, then there would be no need to give D.J. any additional details.

"I need to find out who visited Moana while she was in prison," Sione said. "Could you find that out?"

"Why would you want to find out who visited her while she was in prison?" D.J. asked. "And wait a minute. Did you just say her name? I thought *Moana* was a curse from hell. Since when did you start saying her name?"

"Since she died."

"What?" D.J. stared at him. "She died?"

"Moana is dead."

"How did she die?" D.J. asked. "Was she sick?"

"She was killed in a prison fight."

"A prison fight?"

"There was some kind of riot," Sione said. "And she was stabbed, but ..."

"But?"

"But I'm not sure that's true." Sione sighed, rubbing his jaw. "I know this will sound crazy, but I think maybe the prison riot was arranged so that her death would look like an accident."

"Arranged? You mean like somebody had Moana killed?"

Reluctant, Sione said, "Maybe."

"Why would you think that?"

"You remember I told you she was calling me," Sione said. "Well, she didn't feel safe in prison. She said somebody had threatened to kill her."

"Who threatened her?" D.J. asked.

"I'd rather not say," Sione said, looking away from his cousin's shrewd scrutiny. "So, do you think you could get the information for me?"

"I'll see what I can do," D.J. said. "But ..."

Wary, Sione glanced at his cousin. "What?"

"Did she tell her lawyer about these threats?" D.J. asked. "Or the warden?"

"I don't know," Sione said. "I don't think so."

"Why did she tell you?" his cousin asked, leaning forward. "What did she think you could do?"

You have to tell Richard not to hurt me.

"She wanted me to talk to the person who threatened her."

"So, the person is someone you know?"

"Yeah," Sione admitted. "That's why I want to see who visited her. I want to see if this person came to see her and threatened her."

"Does this someone have a name?"

Exhaling, Sione rubbed his eyes, already regretting his decision to get D.J. involved.

"Is it Ben Chang?"

Staring at his cousin, Sione said, "Why would you think it was Ben?"

"I know what went down between them," D.J. said, sitting back. "I know you think he set her up, left her holding the bag in that situation they had with the boutique in Jamaica. Maybe she's been making noise about ratting him out to get herself a new trial, or something. And maybe he paid her a visit to tell her that snitching on him would be a bad idea."

Sione leaned forward and rested his elbows on the desk. The idea of letting D.J. think Ben had threatened his ex-fiancée was tempting and not farfetched. Ben and Moana had a tumultuous history. It wouldn't be surprising for Ben to issue a threat to Moana if he thought she was trying to set him up.

Still, Sione didn't want to lie to his cousin. He couldn't tell D.J. the truth though. Not now. And maybe he wouldn't have to, if it turned out that Richard hadn't visited Moana.

"Let me ask you this," D.J. said. "If your suspicions about Ben are true, then what are you going to do?"

"I'm not sure," Sione said. "Before I do anything, I need to find out who visited her in prison."

Ask your father.

Ben's taunt floated in his head, but Sione prayed it wouldn't get to that point. If at all possible, he wanted to avoid any face-to-face contact with Richard.

8

Disgruntled and leery, her nerves on edge, Spencer swatted at a mosquito flying near her nose and tried to concentrate as the guide gave an overview of the tour.

Under the bright and hot early morning sun, fourteen tourists from five different hotels gathered in a haphazard circle in front of the tour bus, a large sixty-plus-passenger vehicle painted bright green with colorful caricatures of smiling jungle animals surrounded by rainforest.

They'd just gotten off the bus after a forty-five-minute drive from the heart of San Ignacio and were now being thanked for choosing Angie's Eco-Adventure's Cave-O-Rama, which promised the exploration of four different caves in about eight hours with scheduled stops for refreshment and lunch.

Behind her dark Prada sunglasses, Spencer rolled her eyes. She was absolutely not in the mood for cave exploration, but she hadn't chosen this damn tour.

Just like the tour a few days ago to the Mayan ruins, the cave tour had been the bright idea of Ben, who expected her to use the excursion as a cover for another Xanax box delivery. But unlike the trip to Xunantunich, when she'd been told to leave the pink beach bag on the bus so some strange woman could take it, the plan for the cave tour was slightly different. Sighing, Spencer swatted another mosquito and forced herself to listen to the tour guide. Enthusiastic and agile, the guide engaged the group warmly, introducing herself and giving them a bit of information about her experiences as a tour guide in Belize, a job she'd been doing for more than ten years.

As the guide went over the safety instructions and made sure everyone was properly clothed—long, loose-fitting pants and shirts, hiking shoes—Spencer's mind raced. Thoughts scattered, she fixated on one thing, then became obsessed with another, and then dwelled on yet another thing.

Her stomach jumped, thinking about what she had to do, wondering if she would be able to pull it off. *Part One* of the side venture had gone fine, but her success didn't give her confidence. If anything, she worried her luck would run out. What would happen if she made a stupid mistake? Ben's instructions had come via the cab driver, and who knew if the sweaty, smarmy fool had relayed them correctly? Just like when she'd been on the Mayan tour, Spencer felt paranoid and figured she was being watched.

"Everybody ready?" the guide said, smiling. "C'mon, let's go!"

Hot and humid, the sun was too bright, and Spencer was too damn pissed and terrified to care about the series of caves she was about to visit on this particular excursion. She faked as much enthusiasm as she could and headed off with the group into the first cave.

An hour later, Spencer had already had quite enough of stalagmites and stalactites. But the tour was called Cave-O-Rama, and so after a respite of water and a protein bar, they were herded back on the bus and quickly got back on the road.

At the second cave, Spencer followed the guide, who led them on a steep downward slope. Struggling to keep her footing over the uneven cave floor and loose rocks, she felt as though they were headed down into the bowels of the earth. As the light from the opening began to fade and darkness converged, flashlights winked to life, their beams splaying across the cave walls, illuminating what the tour guide said were crystalline formations.

At the third cave, the guide led them along the cave floor, a long, wide stretch of uneven, broken stone formations. Spencer stared up at the stalactites hanging from the ceiling as the guide explained that the cave had been used by the Mayans as a burial site.

As the day wore on, Spencer found herself forgetting her fears and troubles. Her eyes began to adjust more quickly to the gloom. The no-see-ums became less annoying. The tour guide's overexcitement lost some of its irritation, and she allowed herself to be entertained and informed.

The fourth cave featured vaulted openings, which allowed light to stream in. Spencer cut her flashlight off and kept pace with a group of energetic geriatrics as they crossed a footbridge to the exit. By the time the tour was over, she realized she'd enjoyed it and was looking forward to calling Shady to give her the details.

After the last cave, the bright, colorful tour bus pulled off the road and turned into a rest area. It was a large park operated and maintained by some government tourism association. Gravel pathways snaked between the manicured lawns. There were lots of trees, several corrugated buildings, an information center, a gift shop, and washroom facilities.

Two dozen tourists got off the bus, stretching their legs. Famished and fatigued, they clustered around the tour guide, who corralled everyone toward a large, wide tent under which there were several picnic tables.

The sun was directly overhead, beaming down like a hot, glaring spotlight, but Spencer was glad for the heat and brightness after the shadowy, dark dampness of the caves.

Crowding beneath the welcomed shade, the tourists grabbed paper plates and began to partake of the cold sandwiches, fruit, chips, cookies, and water that were spread out, buffet style, on one of the tables. Spencer's stomach grumbled.

According to the website, lunch would be provided at the end of the tour, which was when the cab driver had told her to make the delivery. Separating herself from the group, she hurried along the gravel path toward the restroom. In her mind, she rehearsed the instructions.

Go to the restroom. Go to the handicapped stall. An OUT OF ORDER sign will be on the door. Go inside the handicapped stall. There should be a green beach bag on the hook on the door. Take that green bag. Leave your green bag with the money and passports on the hook. Then leave.

Spencer didn't like the plan. Too many things could go wrong. What about other tourists coming into the restroom? The group was comprised mainly of the very old and the very young. Historically, little kids and geezers had weak bladders and were always rushing to pee. What if someone asked a worker to fix the broken toilet? What if somebody stole the green bag? What if she was spotted going into or coming out of the broken toilet stall?

Spencer slipped behind the door marked LADIES. Inside, it was cool, well lit, and surprisingly clean. More sanitary than she'd expected. Four stalls. Three separate pedestal basins, each with a mirror above it.

After checking to make sure the restroom was empty, she walked to the handicapped stall, saw the "Out of Order" sign, and pushed the door open. Spencer went into the stall, closed the door behind her, locked it, and turned. She stared at the hook.

No green beach bag. *Damn!* Spencer was pissed but not surprised. Hadn't she known something would go wrong? What the hell was she going to do? She had to think of something. But why should she? Ben didn't want her to think. He just wanted her to look pretty and do his bidding. She would call him, she decided. Tell him the bag hadn't been in the handicapped stall and ask him what he wanted her to do.

Resolved, Spencer opened the stall door. A girl stood in front of her, blocking her. Spencer stammered her apologies and then rushed out of the stall, accidentally shoulder-checking the freckled-faced girl as she hurried toward the door.

"Not so fast, black Barbie."

Black Barbie? Strange images filtered into her mind. A dismembered doll on the floor. Head, arms, and legs ripped from the torso and—

Startled, Spencer pushed the intrusive memory away and then faced the girl, not sure what to think or if she should be offended. "Do I know you?"

"You don't need to know me," the young woman said. "All you need to do is follow the instructions Ben Chang gave you."

Ben Chang. Frowning, Spencer stared at the girl, skeptical. This freckle-faced tomboy knew Ben? This kid with her big blue innocent eyes had some connection to a Jamaican businessman with vague criminal ties? Hard to believe, and somehow, Spencer wasn't surprised.

Annoyed, and yet relieved to be finished with the second side venture, Spencer removed the green bag from her shoulder. "Guess this is for you," Spencer said, noticing the slightly darker green bag strapped across the freckle-faced girl's boyish frame.

Spencer tossed the green bag onto the pedestal basin closest to the handicapped stall, then turned, and headed for the door. Technically, the instructions were to trade beach bags, but she wasn't in the mood for cloak and dagger foolishness and didn't think it was necessary to—

"Stop right there," the tomboy said. "Turn around."

Apprehensive, Spencer looked over her shoulder at the girl. The blue eyes were no longer innocent, but threatening, and her scowl was a fitting accompaniment to the gun she pointed at Spencer. Stomach twisting, Spencer tried to ignore the jolt of fear slicing through her. Was this woman really pointing a gun at her? This kid, really, with bright yellow nail polish and a cheap silver butterfly ring on her pinky finger was pointing a gun at her.

"Don't try nothing stupid," the blonde tomboy said. "You're a good-looking woman. You don't want to get shot in the face."

Shot in the face. The idea terrified Spencer, but it annoyed her too. Was this really her life right now? Had all the bad decisions and stupid mistakes really led her to this moment where she was standing in a bathroom in some Central American country while a woman held a gun on her, threatening to shoot her? The worst part was she had brought all of this on herself. She wouldn't be in this position if she hadn't made the stupid mistake of dating Ben.

"Get away from the door," the tomboy ordered, her voice shaking just like the big, black gun in her small, pale hand. "Go stand in front of the handicapped stall."

Spencer did as she was told while the tomboy walked backward to the door. Keeping her gaze and her gun on Spencer, she locked the restroom door. The tomboy went to the basin where Spencer had thrown the beach bag, scooped it up, and then threw it down at Spencer's feet.

"You don't have to point a gun at me," Spencer said. "I'm giving you the bag."

"I need to make sure that bag contains what was promised to me," the tomboy said. "I need to make sure Ben didn't decide to cheat me. I don't trust that bastard."

"What did he promise you?"

"A chance to stay alive," the woman said.

Wary, Spencer said, "A chance to stay alive? What does that mean?"

"It means I don't want to die," the blonde tomboy said. "So, going with the devil I know is better than taking a chance on the devil I don't."

"What is all of this about?" Spencer persisted, irritated by the blonde's cryptic evasiveness. "Why is Ben giving you this money? Is it payment for something you did for him? Or payment to stay quiet about something?"

"Ben wants me to go against Richard," the blonde said. "It's dangerous, but ..."

"Who is Richard?" Spencer asked, trying to recall if Ben had ever mentioned the name.

"Richard is the Goddamn devil," the blonde said. "And when Richard finds out what I've done, I'm going to be dead to him. Ben said he could make sure that Richard can't get to me. Not that I trust Ben, because I don't. Ben is not really trying to save my ass, he's trying to get back at Richard."

"Why is Ben trying to get back at Richard?" Spencer asked.

The blonde frowned, suspicion in her blue eyes. Spencer wasn't sure if the tomboy was wary of her questions or skeptical about her own rambling, maybe realizing she'd said more than she should have or more than she'd wanted to.

"No more questions," the blonde said. "Open the bag. Slowly. And then dump everything out of the box. Put everything on the floor where I can see it."

Spencer complied, removing five stacks of money and a passport. Crouching, she arranged everything on the floor, in a line, for the tomboy's inspection.

"So, did he keep his promise?" Spencer asked and then stood.

"Seems he did," the tomboy said. "But …"

"But …?"

"What's the name on the passport?"

Spencer bent down, grabbed the passport, and opened it. "Helen Johnson."

"Helen?" the tomboy made a face, her blue eyes troubled, wistful.

She seemed very young and naïve, as if she should be in some frilly pink bedroom gossiping about boys while she did her nails, not holding a gun and complaining about the name on a fake passport.

How the hell had she gotten mixed up with Ben Chang? Had she made a stupid mistake and ended up indebted to him, forced to do a favor, or something even worse?

"You don't like the name Helen?"

"It's kind of old-fashioned." The tomboy who was soon to become Helen Johnson shrugged. "Guess it really doesn't matter though."

Except, Spencer suspected, it did matter, more than the tomboy would ever admit. It wasn't that she didn't like the name Helen. She didn't want to be Helen Johnson.

"So, now what?" Spencer asked, anxious to see if she was right about the reason behind the tomboy's hesitation. "You're just going to become Helen Johnson? You're just going to leave who you really are behind? How can you do that? How can you just give up yourself and become someone else?"

"I have no choice." The tomboy scowled and then dropped to one knee in front of the money. "Can't get on the bad side of Ben Chang. That's a dangerous place to be. Not going to end up like Livvie."

"Livvie?" Spencer asked. "Who is that?"

"Olivia Eastman," the tomboy said. "We worked together."

"Where?"

"Place called Kwik Kash."

"Kwik Kash," Spencer said, familiar with the company. "Ben owns that, right?"

Nodding, the blonde said, "Yeah. Well, he did. But it burned down. The cops said Livvie did it. Supposedly, she stole a bunch of money from the Kwik Kash safe then set the place on fire to cover up the crime and accidentally got trapped in the building and burned herself alive, but that's not true."

Spencer glanced at the blonde. "What really happened to Olivia?"

"Richard killed her. Then burned her body up to cover up what he'd done," the tomboy said. "That's what I think, anyway."

"Did you tell the police?"

The blonde's head jerked up and she scowled at Spencer. "Are you crazy? You think I have a death wish? You think I want to be shot in the head then burned to death?"

As the blonde tomboy grabbed stacks of the money and shoved them back into the Xanax box, Spencer shuddered despite the balmy atmosphere in the ladies room. She didn't want to hear any more of the grisly story and regretted asking for details. Engaging the blonde in conversation had been a mistake, but she had to know why Ben was providing the woman with money and a fake passport.

She'd been too curious. Now she knew things she didn't want to know, things she didn't know how to deal with. Ben was more dangerous than she'd realized or could have ever imagined. Curiosity, she scoffed to herself. No wonder they said it killed the cat.

The tomboy tossed the gun into the green beach bag, hoisted it on her thin shoulder, then turned, and rushed to the door.

"Wait, before you go," Spencer said. "Tell me your real name."

The pale, freckle-faced girl turned to Spencer and frowned.

"My real name …" The tomboy faltered, her eyes bright and glassy as she bit her lip.

Spencer waited, holding her breath, anxious. She wasn't sure why she wanted to know the tomboy's name, but for some reason, it was important to her.

Shaking her head, the tomboy regarded her with guarded, suspicious eyes. "My name is Helen Johnson."

9

San Ignacio, Belize
Belizean Banyan Resort - Honeymoon Casita

"How are you, sweet girl?"

Spencer rolled over onto her back, staring at the ceiling above the king-sized bed as she clutched the burner phone. She wasn't in the mood to deal with Ben Chang, but it wouldn't be a good idea to ignore the calls of a man who could have her arrested. She glanced at the clock on the bedside table. A few minutes after midnight.

When he hadn't called earlier, she'd decided he would contact her tomorrow for a full report about the cave tour. Settling between the plush bed linens, she'd curled into a ball, letting her mind wander as she dozed and thought about the things the blonde tomboy had told her.

Ben wants me to go against Richard.

When Richard finds out what I've done, I'm going to be dead to him.

Ben is not really trying to save my ass. He's trying to get back at Richard.

It was as if she had pieces to a puzzle, but she wasn't sure how to fit the pieces together or if the pieces even belonged to the same puzzle.

After the tour bus dropped her off in front of the resort, Spencer had returned to the honeymoon casita, poured a glass of wine, and then called her sisters to update them on the day's events. Two hours later, she, Shady, and Rae were confused by the blonde tomboy's story, and they'd concluded there were too many unanswered questions.

Who the hell was Richard? Why did Ben want the tomboy to go against Richard? Why was Ben trying to get back at Richard?

Following the conversation with her sisters, questions about Ben and Richard faded, and thoughts of "Helen Johnson" plagued her.

Spencer had asked the freckle-faced girl how she could abandon who she really was and become someone she wasn't. There had been blatant condemnation in her tone. How could she judge? Spencer had done the same thing when she'd agreed to start "dating."

She'd willingly given up the person she really was to become some strange, alternate version of herself. A version she didn't recognize. A version of herself she was ashamed of and hated. And for what? To pay the rent? To keep the lights on? To put food on the table?

"Dating" was supposed to have given her freedom.

So, how had she ended up trapped in this nightmare?

She'd been wondering if she would always have to pay for the stupid mistakes she'd made when the damn burner phone rang.

No rest for the weary or the wicked. And she was both.

"I'm tired," she said, answering his question. "I've had a long, difficult day, and I just want to go to sleep. So, I know you're calling to find out how the cave tour went."

"And how was it?"

Sitting up, she arranged the pillows behind her. "Just as fun and exciting as the Mayan ruins."

"No problems?"

Spencer hesitated, debating whether or not to tell him about the gun "Helen Johnson" had pointed at her but quickly decided he probably wouldn't give a damn anyway.

"No problems," she said. "Everything went fine."

"Good job, sweet girl."

Spencer took the phone from her ear and then gave it the finger. Ben hadn't seen her obscene gesture, but flipping him off was cathartic and had accomplished what three glasses of wine, a two-hour conversation with her sisters, and a long, hot bath hadn't been able to. She finally felt some of the tension coiled within her begin to unwind.

"Only one more side venture to do," Ben said. "I'll be in touch with your instructions. Until then, you can focus your efforts on *Step Two*. Get the dinner invitation."

"I understand what I have to do," she said. "Now, are we finished with this conversation? Because it's past my bed time."

"I hope you do understand what I expect from you, sweet girl," Ben said. "I hope you don't disappoint me."

10

"Who're the cupcakes for?" Ms. Edwards asked.

"My cousin's little girls." Sione made a few uneven, haphazard swirls around the circumference of the chocolate cupcake he'd been half-ass frosting when Spencer Edwards knocked on the door of his casita a few minutes ago, claiming she needed to talk to him.

"They look good."

"You want one?"

"Not really," Ms. Edwards said, walking over toward the table before pivoting gracefully and heading back toward the island.

"Okay then, what can I help you with?" he asked, staring at her.

She looked so beautiful, he had to force himself to remember he still wasn't sure if she was involved in some sort of crime or not. For the past few days, he'd been thinking about the situation with Spencer Edwards from the day she arrived, complaining about the honeymoon casita, to the report D.J. had given him about her last excursion, when she'd taken a cave exploring tour.

D.J. had called it another interesting day. His cousin had narrated Ms. Edwards' cave tour trip, and as Sione stared at the accompanying photos, he found himself, once again, entranced by her beauty. There were no bad pictures. Each frame showcased her delicate, flawless features.

When the tour was over, Ms. Edwards had gone into the restroom. D.J. had called his attention to Ms. Edwards' Kelly green beach bag. A few minutes later, a thin woman with blonde hair pulled back into a ponytail entered the facilities. She was also carrying a beach bag, though hers was moss green.

About fifteen minutes later, the blonde woman exited the restroom carrying the Kelly green bag Spencer had been carrying. Then Spencer Edwards came out of the bathroom, and on her shoulder was the moss green beach bag the blonde woman had been carrying when she'd entered the restroom.

Ms. Edwards and the blonde woman had switched bags, obviously. Sione didn't want to believe it and didn't know what to think.

D.J. had followed the blonde woman back to her hotel. In addition to finding out her name—Karen Nelson—he'd also managed to take a few close-up shots of her. Karen Nelson's freckled image on the picture D.J. had taken was the same thumbnail photo on one of the passports Sione had made a copy of—the passport with the name "Helen Johnson."

Karen Nelson had arrived in Belize a week ago from San Diego, California, D.J. had learned, and she had an interesting employment history. A few weeks ago, Karen Nelson had been a senior teller at a small, family-owned bank. Before that, she'd worked at Kwik Kash with Carla Garcia—the woman who'd gotten off the tour bus with Ms. Edwards' pink beach bag.

"And Ms. Nelson had a record, too," D.J. had said. "Busted for writing hot checks."

Because Carla Garcia and Karen Nelson had been co-workers at Kwik Kash, D.J. believed the women were involved in some sort of financial scheme. Whatever the crime, his cousin was convinced Ms. Edwards was right in the thick of it. She wasn't some clueless girl who didn't know what she was transporting but a willing participant in the malfeasance with informed consent.

Staring at Ms. Edwards, Sione was inclined to believe she was more than just a pretty girl involved in some scam. She was complicated, frustrating, and maybe too alluring, too enticing, for him to ignore or resist. But he had to resist her. Getting involved with a woman like Spencer Edwards would cause him more harm than good, he was sure of that.

"What can you help me with? Did you really just ask me that? You can help me by finding my damn manuals!"

"I am working on that," Sione said, forcing himself to focus on decorating the cupcakes and not on how good she looked in the black dress she wore, particularly the top part which had a plunging neckline that struggled to contain her breasts.

"Still working on it? I don't understand. How hard is it to find the idiot who delivered the wrong box?"

He looked up from the cupcakes to stare at her. "Ms. Edwards, I assure you, I will take care of this situation."

"If you take care of the situation with my missing manuals the way you took care of the man who attacked me," she said, frowning in a way he found much too tempting, "then I'm sure I'll never see those manuals again."

"What the hell do your missing manuals have to do with the man who attacked you?"

"You're going to let that idiot delivery guy get away with delivering the wrong box just like you let that Asian guy get away with attacking me!"

Confused, he looked at her. "Ms. Edwards, I stopped him from attacking you."

"And then you let him escape!" Ms. Edwards said. "You beat the crap out of him for nothing!"

Sione didn't want to think about what he'd done to the Asian guy. He regretted his violence and was ashamed of how satisfied and satiated he'd felt when the guy was crumpled in a heap on the ground.

"I never should have come to this damn resort," she said. "You can count on me giving you a scathing negative review."

Sighing, he looked at her. "Ms. Edwards, I don't think I can adequately express to you how sorry I am that someone broke into your casita and about this mishap with your manuals, but I really want to make things right and—"

"Do you really?" she asked, an odd dare in her tone.

Wary of the slight predatory gleam in her gaze, he said, "Of course, I do. As I told you, it's very important that all my guests have the most relaxing, pleasant experience during their stay at the Belizean Banyan."

"If you mean what you say," she said, "then I think we can find a way to rectify the situation. But I don't have time to talk right now— I'm going snorkeling—so, maybe we can—"

A riot of giggles floated through the kitchen, carefree and effervescent, followed by a loud Sssshhhh and then more giggles.

Sione scanned the kitchen, focusing on the huge, round table, noticing movement beneath it, small figures scrambling, scurrying.

"What the hell," Sione said under his breath, walking around the island and heading toward the table.

Squealing and giggling, the figures emerged from beneath the table. Ms. Edwards gasped as three little girls scrambled across the kitchen, waving and making teasing kissing noises and laughing.

"Keisha, India, Maggie!" Sione shouted. "Come back here!"

"Are those ..." Spencer Edwards looked at him. "Your little girls?"

"They're my cousin's kids," Sione sighed. "I'm babysitting. Listen, I need to find them before they tear up the casita."

11

San Ignacio, Belize

Belizean Banyan Resort - Owner's Casita

"Hey, you know what we should do?" Ms. Edwards said, her tone conspiratorial as she motioned to his little cousins to join her on the couch, which they happily did, squealing and giggling, still in the throes of a sugar high after all the cupcakes they'd had. "We should go jump in Sione's bed!"

From his position on the floor, where he'd crashed in a heap after a particularly vigorous game of hide-and-seek with Ms. Edwards and his energetic little cousins, Sione struggled to sit up. "Huh?"

"Yeah!" the girls shouted, clapping their hands. "Let's jump in Sione's bed!"

Groggy, Sione fought to clear his head. *Let's jump in Sione's bed? What the hell?* "Wait, wait," Sione protested. "No, jumping in Sione's bed is not—"

"Last one to the bed is a rotten plantain!" Ms. Edwards declared.

When Sione had run out of the kitchen earlier, chasing after his mischievous second cousins, Ms. Edwards had done something strange and unexpected. She'd followed him, heading out of the kitchen behind him, announcing her plans to come with him and join in the search. Sione hadn't rebuffed her offer. Actually, he'd been intrigued and excited by her willingness to tag along.

Staggering to his feet, Sione ran a hand down the back of his head. Would the girls ever fall asleep? Why weren't they tired? Why wasn't Ms. Edwards tired? The hide-and-seek, the charades, the piggyback rides, and the musical chairs had just about wiped him out, plus his head was pounding and his stomach was grumbling.

But Ms. Edwards was still empowered with the same endless energy that had his cousin's daughters bouncing off the walls. And yet, it was interesting, a bit exciting, to see a silly, playful side of Ms. Edwards.

Up until today, he'd only witnessed her deliberate abrasiveness, but as he'd watched her interactions with the girls, it was hard to reconcile the fierce badass with the vibrant, lovely woman who'd laughed as the girls tried to teach her how to do the samba.

Still, he couldn't ignore the money and fake passports and the excursions she'd taken to possibly deliver that money and those passports to women who formerly worked at Kwik Kash. There was the suspicion of some kind of white-collar shenanigans but still no concrete proof.

D.J. had plenty of photos of Ms. Edwards in which she appeared to have switched beach bags with both Karen Nelson and Carla Garcia. The truth was, they really didn't know what had been inside those bags. Maybe he didn't want to know. Maybe he didn't want to believe Ms. Edwards was caught up in some white-collar crime.

Sione lumbered down the hall and into his room. Ms. Edwards

and his cousins were jumping, laughing, and squealing, using his bed as a trampoline.

"No, no, NO!" Sione strode to the foot of the bed. "Keisha! Maggie! India! Get off the bed! Now!"

He might as well have been speaking Latin for all the attention they were paying him, which was absolutely none as they continued to do cartwheels across the mattress.

"Girls!" Sione shouted, in vain, he knew. They weren't listening; they were busy having a pillow fight, which Ms. Edwards had instigated. "Stop jumping in my bed! Ms. Edwards!"

"Come join us!" Ms. Edwards said, doing a few ballerina moves, which his second cousins tried to copy.

"Ms. Edwards," Sione said. "I think if you stop jumping, they'll stop jumping."

"Oh, you're no fun!" she said, sticking out her tongue at him.

"You're no fun, Sione!" the girls chorused. "You're no fun!"

Sione closed his eyes, counted to ten, and told himself it wouldn't make sense to explode. As he tried to counter the frustration rising in his chest, he was aware of the bedsprings creaking and the headboard hitting the wall. If not for the laughter, it might be the sound of someone in his bed having wild, rigorous sex. He opened his eyes, and the first thing he noticed was that every time Ms. Edwards jumped, her dress lifted, exposing her thighs. Quickly, Sione looked away, not willing to get an erection in front of—

A scream slashed through the air, carrying a hint of surprise. The girls shouted in alarm. Startled, Sione glanced toward the bed. Ms. Edwards was flying through the air.

"Miss Spencer!" the girls cried out. "Don't fall!"

Sione rushed to the left side of the bed, catching Ms. Edwards before she bounced off the bed and ended up on the floor on her ass. Laughing, she placed her hands on his shoulders and wiggled out of his arms, sliding down the length of his body, staring at him with just enough restrained lust to send him over the edge, while the feel of her breasts, her intoxicating fragrance, and the heat from her flushed skin had him as hard as concrete.

The girls giggled, whispering and pointing. Sione looked at them, confused. Ms. Edwards gasped, and seconds later, Sione realized why. That slow, sensuous trip along his body had caused her dress to ride up toward her stomach, exposing her black lace panties.

"Well, ladies," Ms. Edwards said, standing in front of him, blocking his current condition while she engaged in a furious attempt to smooth her dress down. "I think it might be time for me to leave."

12

After a quick breakfast of toast and yogurt, most of which had gone uneaten, Spencer called the front desk to request a cab. She was tired and exhausted from lack of sleep. Last night, because of Ben Chang, she'd had to deal with a stark, paralyzing fear she hadn't had to contend with in almost fifteen years.

He'd called to give her instructions for the third and, supposedly, final, "side venture" he wanted her to do, and before ending the call, Ben had warned her again not to disappoint him.

For some reason, the idea of disappointing him had taken her back to a time in her life she didn't like to remember. Those sad, confusing times when her mother would say, *I'm really disappointed in you,* and Spencer could only guess it was because she'd done something stupid, something wrong, something to make her mother come to the conclusion that she wasn't worth love and attention.

Often, following the declaration of her mother's disappointment in her, there would be slaps, screams, kicks, and shoves. Once her mother grew bored with beating her black and blue, she would order Spencer to go to her room and not come out until she was told to. And then, the front door would slam.

Spencer hated Ben for making her feel like she was seven years old again, when she'd been left alone, too many times to count, in a dirty apartment with little food after her mother had abused her and then headed off to God only knew where.

Back then, she would be fine during the day and a little glad that she didn't have to worry about being smacked across the face. Finding ways to entertain herself, Spencer would read books, color, and play games with the few stuffed animals she had, pretending they were her friends. She would scrounge and forage for food, usually finding peanut butter and saltines or dry cereal.

As morning gave way to afternoon and afternoon yielded to dusk, her panic increased and fear stalked her until darkness came. In the inky blackness, terror claimed her, holding her in its grip until the wispy streaks of dawn stretched across the floor and flooded the room with warmth and light. Only then would she allow herself to relax, to unclench her fists and go limp, her jaw slackening as sleep took her into a dreamless unconsciousness.

This morning, Spencer had woken up angry, frustrated, and more than a little sad, thinking about her seven-year-old-self. But there was no time for tears. She couldn't disappoint Ben. She had to do the side venture for him.

Sighing, Spencer checked her watch. Where the hell was that damn cab? Hadn't she called twenty minutes ago? Frustrated, Spencer grabbed a white oversized beach bag with the Belizean Banyan logo and checked the contents. Wallet. Sunglasses. Sun screen. Lip gloss. Burner phone. And the box of anti-anxiety meds, which contained five bundles of money and a fake passport, the items to deliver while she was in San Pedro.

A few minutes later, Spencer left the casita and made her way to the hotel lobby. Stomping to the front desk, she rolled her eyes when she saw Analee, the idiot desk assistant.

"Where the hell is the taxi I called for an hour ago?" Spencer demanded.

Of course, the idiot desk assistant gave her a blank stare before stammering some lame excuse.

"I'm not in the mood for apologies," Spencer snapped. "Just get me a damn taxi, now."

While Spencer was complaining to Analee about her deplorable incompetence, Sione Tuiali'i walked over, butting in where he had no damn business. Spencer suspected the desk assistant had alerted him, somehow, maybe pushed a "panic" button beneath her keyboard.

As usual, the resort owner was irritatingly tall, handsome, and muscular, and even though he was wearing a tan short-sleeved polo, she couldn't help but remember how he'd looked with his shirt off. Despite his mesmerizing good looks, Spencer felt conflicted when she saw him. His presence reminded her of the "favor" Ben wanted her to do.

Step Two. Sweet girl gets close to the resort owner.

Sione was willing and eager to help with the misunderstanding. Spencer felt spiteful and wanted to tell him she didn't need his assistance, but she knew the more encounters she had with him, the greater her chances of successfully completing *Step Two*.

After telling Analee he would take care of the situation, Sione steered Spencer toward a small alcove, away from the other guests. "Explain to me what happened."

"Your desk assistant was supposed to call a cab for me," Spencer said. "But she didn't, and because of her incompetence, I have been waiting for almost two hours!"

"I'm sorry about that."

Spencer rolled her eyes. "I doubt that very seriously."

"Ms. Edwards," he said. "It's very important to me that my guests have everything they need to have a pleasant stay here at the resort."

"That's what you keep saying."

"And that's what I mean," he said. "Which is why I am going to take you wherever it is that you need to go."

"You are?" She stared up at him, shocked. "I mean, you would be willing to do that? Because I'm going to San Pedro to buy souvenirs."

"I don't mind at all," Sione said. "I would be happy to take you to San Pedro."

Spencer was a bit suspicious of his offer, but the damn sincerity in his hazel eyes was too intense. And, of course, time alone with him might help her complete *Step Two*. She couldn't turn him down.

An hour later, they were headed to Ambergris Caye, the largest island on Belize, a trip over land and sea from the resort to the pier downtown, where they took an island ferry to San Pedro.

As the ferry sped closer to the island, the turquoise Caribbean gave way to powdery white sand stretching toward a row of buildings in creamy pastel colors. Hundreds of tourists milled about, mixing with vendors and business owners hawking their various and sundry wares beneath a cloudless blue sky and a warm, brilliant sun.

In the town of San Pedro, Spencer and the tall handsome resort owner walked parallel to the beach, strolling past a variety of restaurants and shops, making small talk and looking at souvenirs.

Fifteen minutes later, she told him she wanted to go to a boutique she'd read about on the Internet. He knew about the shop and was able to steer her toward a small, quaint place with inviting pale yellow walls and hardwood floors. It was a boutique designed for tourists with dozens of racks of resort wear—flirty sundresses, bikinis, T-shirts, shorts, and sarongs—all in a variety of appealing prints and colors.

After picking out a few sarongs and sundresses, Spencer went into the dressing room. When an attendant came by to offer help, Spencer said, "Oh, thank you, but Maxine was helping me. Can you please tell her I need some assistance?"

The boutique attendant hurried off to find Maxine.

Moments later, Spencer was trying on a strapless turquoise sundress when she heard, "You need some help?"

Startled for a moment, Spencer took a breath and pulled the curtain back.

"Maxine Porter," the woman said, extending a hand.

"Hi," Spencer said, giving Maxine a quick handshake, wondering why the woman was acting as though they were business associates at some convention and not two stupid women forced to do the bidding of Ben Chang. "Spencer Edwards."

"So, Spencer, do you have meds for me?"

"Yes, I do," Spencer said, trying to sound cheerful as she reached down and grabbed the Belizean Banyan beach bag.

"That's where you're staying?" Maxine asked. "The Belizean Banyan?"

Spencer nodded, noting the grudging admiration and jealousy crossing the woman's features.

"Nice." Maxine took the Xanax. "You must be really special to Ben. He usually doesn't put a girl up in such an expensive place unless he really likes her."

Nonplussed, Spencer stared at Maxine, not sure what to think. She was special to Ben? Spencer rolled her eyes and grabbed a cotton-candy-colored sarong to try on. *Yeah, right.* There was no way she was special to Ben. Not the way he treated her. If she were so damn special to him, he wouldn't be forcing her to do these damn favors.

"Used for the relief of anxiety," Maxine said, reading the box. "I have been pretty anxious these days."

"What is all this about?" Spencer asked.

"It's about staying alive," Maxine Porter said, looking away. "Ben is trying to save my life."

"Trying to save your life?" Spencer stared at the woman. "I don't understand. Are you in danger or something?"

"Or something."

"Or something?" Spencer prompted, anxious for real answers, not just vague, guarded responses. "Please, tell me what is going on?"

"The devil wants me dead," Maxine said, smirking.

Spencer shrank back, disturbed. "What?"

Maxine gave Spencer a wink before she turned.

"Wait," Spencer grabbed the woman's elbow.

Maxine looked back, her gaze dropping to Spencer's hand, gripping her arm. "What do you want?"

Spencer drew her hand back and said, "You said that the devil wants you dead."

Maxine stared at her, suspicion in her dark eyes.

Remembering the tomboy's words, Spencer asked, "Were you talking about Richard?"

"You know Richard?"

Shaking her head, Spencer said, "I'm just trying to figure out what's going on. I delivered some medicine to a blonde girl a few days ago, and she told me that Ben wanted her to go against Richard. She said Ben wanted to get back at Richard, and that was why Ben had given her the money and passport. But she didn't say why Ben wanted to get back at Richard."

"And you want me to tell you?"

Spencer sighed and said, "I just want to understand what's going on."

"Why? What does it matter to you?" Maxine asked.

"It matters because the blonde girl told me that Richard killed some woman and then—"

"Olivia." Maxine cut in. "She worked with us at Kwik Kash. It was the four of us. Me, Karen—the blonde you delivered to on the cave tour—and Carla, who you delivered to on that Mayan tour."

"And Ben gave y'all money and a fake passport because ..." Spencer hoped Maxine would take up the conversation and explain what the hell was going on, so she could understand how and why she was tangled up in this beef between Ben and Richard.

Rolling her eyes, Maxine shook her head. "You know, Ben gave you a specific job to do. He didn't tell you to ask questions about things that don't concern you."

"But it does concern me," Spencer said. "Ben put me in the middle of all this mess when he forced me to be his delivery girl."

"Forced you?"

Spencer glanced down for a moment, pissed at her slip, and then back at Maxine. "I'm not a willing participant. And I don't think you, Karen, and Carla are, either."

Maxine let out a long exhale full of weariness and frustration and then said, "Actually, we were willing participants."

"Willing participants in what?"

"About a year ago, Kwik Kash was investigated by the Feds," Maxine said. "Suspicion of money laundering."

"Money laundering?"

"You seem surprised," Maxine said. "You know that's what Ben does, right? He launders money."

"I knew he wasn't a legitimate businessman," Spencer said, feeling stupid and naïve, not knowing the truth about Ben. How could she have been so dumb? How could she have not had a damn clue?

"Kwik Kash is just a front for the laundry Ben and Richard run together," Maxine said. "It's like their family business."

"Ben and Richard are related?"

"Not by blood. But Ben is like a son to Richard. And Richard is the father Ben never had. Anyway, during the investigation, some special agents approached Olivia," Maxine said. "And she agreed to testify against Richard and Ben. She didn't want to rat, but the Feds really didn't give her a choice. Anyway, Richard found out about the deal Olivia made with the cops and he killed her. Then he set the Kwik Kash on fire—with Olivia's dead body inside."

"Oh my God."

"The Feds found out what happened to Olivia," Maxine said. "So then they approached me, Karen, and Carla because we know all the dirty little secrets about Kwik Kash. They offered us a deal. Immunity in exchange for our testimony against Ben and Richard."

"But, y'all didn't take the deal," Spencer guessed.

"After the Feds came to us," Maxine said. "Richard had a talk with us. And he told us, point blank, you rat, you die. So, me, Karen, and Carla assured Richard that we were not about to snitch on him. Well, a few days later, we have a talk with Ben, and he tells us that Richard doesn't trust us. Ben says Richard wants us dead because Richard thinks the Feds will force us to testify like they forced Olivia. Then Ben tells us he's going to make sure Richard doesn't kill us."

"And you believed him?" Spencer asked.

"The thing was, Ben was beyond pissed at Richard for killing Olivia," Maxine said. "Ben and Olivia had kind of a thing. They were on-again, off-again. Ben and Richard had a bad argument about Olivia, and they kind of fell out about it. Richard is all about loyalty and obedience. He expected Ben to go along with the decision to kill

Olivia because the way Richard saw it, he was doing what was best for Ben. Richard saw killing Olivia as making sure that Ben stayed out of jail. So when Ben got pissed about Olivia's death, Richard wasn't just mad, he was hurt and disappointed."

"So you believe Ben will help you because he's mad about what Richard did to Olivia?"

"Ben is being defiant by helping us," Maxine said. "He's trying to let Richard know that he won't be controlled or ordered around. It's father and son bullshit. But Ben's act of disobedience is going to keep us alive. The money and the new passports will help us get away from Richard. Help us start a new life."

Moments later, after Maxine left the dressing room, Spencer sank down on the bench, disquieted and a bit terrified. She didn't know what to think. Maxine's story was a crazy, twisted tale of death and defiance.

Her own crazy, twisted experiences with Ben had convinced her not to trust him. Maxine was a fool for thinking the passport and the money wouldn't come with strings attached. But to hear Karen and Maxine tell it, Richard was worse than Ben. Both Maxine and Karen had referred to him as a devil. Still, Spencer couldn't help but thinking the women had been forced to choose between the lesser of two evils.

But who was really the lesser evil? Ben? Or Richard?

13

After fifteen minutes, Spencer was fighting frustration. Still confused and disturbed by what Maxine had told her, and needing a distraction, she'd decided to try on the sarong she brought into the dressing room. With the story of betrayal, revenge, and death consuming her thoughts, she couldn't concentrate.

The last side venture was done, and Spencer should have been able to relax, but she felt increasingly angry and afraid that Ben had gotten her involved in the middle of his beef with a guy that both the blonde tomboy and Maxine had called a devil.

Pissed, Spencer yanked the swath of cotton-candy-colored fabric over her head, tossed it on the floor, and plopped down on the cushioned seat across from the full-length mirror in the dressing room.

"Hello," Spencer called out, massaging the spot between her eyes. "Hello. Is there anyone who can help me?"

The privacy curtain was drawn back.

"I'm having a little trouble." Spencer bent over to grab the sarong from the cool, hardwood floor. "I can't—"

"Ms. Edwards."

Spencer froze, still bent at the waist, staring at the floor, trying to ignore the prickly heat rising up her neck and the sound of Sione's voice, which gave her a warm shiver.

"You need help with something?"

"What the hell are you doing in here?"

Standing, struggling to cover herself with the sarong, Spencer took a step back as Sione walked into the dressing room, filling it with his size and strength, crowding her, and a sudden attack of claustrophobia battled with a warm sensation starting deep below her navel and snaking southward toward the center of her thighs.

"Where is the sales lady?"

"I think she's helping another customer," he said.

"Another customer," Spencer mumbled, still trying to cover herself with the swatch of pink fabric. "That figures."

"You need a different size or something?"

"I don't know how to tie this thing." Spencer shook her head. "I've tried and tried."

"Let me help you," Sione said.

"No, no," She said, confused, her mind churning, wondering if she should scream or maybe just let him help her with the sarong. "You don't have to do that, just … I think you should leave."

Smiling, Sione grabbed the sarong from her.

A strange sound erupted from her, something between a squeal and a shriek, as she stood there in her lace bra and matching panties.

"It's actually very easy." He moved behind her.

Spencer's heart thundered. "What are you—"

"Hold up your arms," he instructed, the low timbre of his voice reverberating along the surface of her skin, making her flesh tingle.

Flabbergasted by his blatant audacity, she shook her head. "What?! No, I am not—"

Sione maneuvered Spencer's arms and then wrapped the sarong around her. Shell-shocked, she stood stiff as a board as he worked with the sarong, twisting the ends, bringing them up and behind her neck, and tying them together.

"Okay, there you go." He turned her toward the mirror.

"Hmm," Spencer mumbled, turning to the side, admiring his handiwork, vaguely wondering how he did it and how he knew how to do it.

"You really know how to put one of these things on."

"I know how to take one off, too." He looked at her through the mirror, his gaze dropping to her breasts.

Clearing her throat, Spencer turned from the mirror. "I just don't know about this color. The pale pink might not work."

"Any color will look good on you," Sione said, his eyes dropping lower. "You have beautiful skin."

Deciding to ignore his compliment, Spencer crossed her arms. "You can leave now."

"You need help taking that off?" he asked, slyness in his seemingly concerned tone.

She took a step back, looking up at him. "I'm perfectly capable of taking it off by myself, thank you."

"I don't mind."

Spencer caught him looking at her, holding her with that hypnotic, hazel stare, and immediately, her body betrayed her. His gaze was irrevocably salacious, as if he wanted to rip the sarong off her and screw her against the wall. Or maybe that was what she was thinking. Nevertheless, it wasn't going to happen. And, anyway, sex while "dating" was against protocol.

"We're thieves," Rae had once told her. "Not whores."

The rule was, when "dating," there could never be any real intimacy, only the suggestive illusion of it.

But she wasn't going to "date" the resort owner, she reminded herself. There would be no GHB or theft of property to be subsequently fenced. Ben had promised she wouldn't have to break any laws.

"Well, I do mind," she said, disappointed by the direction her thoughts. "So, can you please get the hell out of here?"

After another cryptic smile, Sione said, "Actually, I can't."

"What do you mean, you can't?"

He stepped back a bit, looking down at her. "There's a woman who just came into the store, and I don't want to see her. Well, I really don't want her to see me, either."

"A woman you don't want to see just came into the store?" She frowned. "What are you talking about? Why don't you want to see her? Who is she?"

He sighed again and seemed embarrassed. "She's a woman I went out with last month, and it didn't work out, and I'm not in the mood for an awkward encounter, and she's a little high-strung."

"Oh, now I get it." Spencer smiled at him, feeling sassy and mischievous. "You had sex with this woman, and then you slipped away before the sun came up, and you never called her again, and you're afraid she's gonna go psycho bitch if she sees you."

"Not exactly." He frowned. "I didn't slip away before the sun came up, but I did tell her I would call her, and I didn't."

"You really think she's gonna pull a fatal attraction because you didn't call her?" Spencer rolled her eyes. "Mr. Tuiali'i, believe it or not, but girls are used to boys not calling when they lie and say they're gonna call."

"I didn't mean to lie to her," he insisted. "I meant to tell her I didn't think it would work out between us."

"But you didn't have the balls to be honest with her," Spencer said, enjoying the look on his handsome face, a combination of shock and indignation. "And since you're still afraid to face her, that tells me you have yet to grow a pair."

He scowled at her. "You're not helping."

"Was I supposed to be?"

"Look, I'll tell you what she looks like and what she's wearing," he said. "You can go out there, and tell me if she's gone. If she's not, then let me know when she leaves the store."

"That's not a good idea."

"Why not?"

"Because you'd have to trust that I was telling the truth if I told you the woman was gone, and who knows if you can trust me?" She gave him another smile. "What if I tricked you? What if I told you the woman was gone, when she really wasn't?"

"You would do that?"

"Who knows?" She shrugged. "Which is why you can't take a chance on me."

He stepped closer to her again, smiling a little. "You don't think I should take a chance on you?"

His gaze wasn't as salacious as it had been moments ago, but it was still suggestive enough to disorient her, make her feel off-kilter, as though the control she'd thought she had was slipping away.

Clearing her throat, she said, "Just tell the girl she must have you mistaken for someone else."

"What?"

"I think you should go back out there," Spencer said. "And if she comes up to you, talking about how you didn't call her, just say, 'I'm sorry, you must have me confused with someone else.'"

"That's not gonna work," he told her. "She's not going to confuse me with someone else."

"I'm telling you what to do," Spencer said. "You say, 'Look, I'm sorry, but, my name is Freddy.'"

He frowned. "Freddy?"

"Isn't that your Belize name or something?" She tried to remember. "You told me that Sione means something in another language."

"I told you that Sione means 'John' in Tongan."

"John." She nodded. "That's right, you did say that. Okay, then say, 'Look, I'm sorry, but my name is John.'"

"I don't want to lie."

"She would rather you lie to her than tell the truth," Spencer said. "You think she really wants to hear that you didn't call her back because you thought she was fugly and you couldn't see yourself screwing her again, by any stretch of anybody's imagination, under any circumstance, even to re-populate the earth following some nuclear catastrophe that only the two of you survived?"

"What the hell?" He shook his head. "That's not what I thought."

"The point is, people don't really want the truth," she said. "They can't handle it."

"That might be true," he conceded. "But I still don't want to lie."

"Then I'll lie for you, *John*."

"What?"

"Let me get dressed, and we'll go out to the sales floor," Spencer said. "I'll make a point to call you *John*, very emphatically, within earshot of this woman. Hopefully, she'll think you're not the guy she thought. But if she does approach you, then I'll tell her your name is *John*, okay?"

Staring down at her, Sione seemed unconvinced of her plan, and as she looked up into his hazel eyes, she wondered if he thought she was a treacherous bitch who used lies to solve her problems.

"Well?" she prompted, trying to forget the disturbing thoughts.

Finally, he nodded. "Okay, fine."

"Okay," Spencer said. *"John."*

Minutes later, Spencer and Sione stood in the middle of the store, which was completely empty, except for two sales associates.

Spencer glanced around the store at the lack of customers milling about the sales racks. "Where is the woman you didn't want to see, *John?"*

Sione cleared his throat, and it seemed he was trying to pretend he wasn't embarrassed. "I guess she must have left."

"You know what, *John,"* Spencer said. "I don't think she was ever in the store."

"You think I made that story up?"

She looked up at him and smiled. "Maybe you did, *John."*

Smiling back, he asked, "And why would I have done that?"

Spencer didn't say anything, just gave him a sly smile. But she thought he was definitely interested, and now there was no more uncertainty, she was no longer unsure. She would be able to get close to him. But not too close, of course. Although, she didn't think she would mind getting a little too close to him.

14

San Ignacio, Belize
Belizean Banyan Resort - Honeymoon Casita

Ms. Edwards kicked her shoes off and plopped down on the couch, staring up at him. "Your uncle left you his entire fortune?"

Sione poured another splash of Blue Label into a shot glass and handed it to her.

After their trip to Ambergris Caye, they'd returned to the resort, and he'd walked Ms. Edwards to her casita. Even after spending most of the day with her—when he should have been working—he didn't want to go back to the lonely owner's casita, where he'd have a myriad of reports waiting to keep him company. He hadn't been ready for his time with her to end, and when she suggested he come in, he didn't hesitate to follow her inside.

"What is this anyway?" She accepted the shot glass. "Did I already ask?"

"Blue Label."

"Nice." She nodded, taking a sniff of the aged malt scotch. "Where'd you get it?"

"We keep it stocked in the bar for our newly married couples."

"Hmmm."

"Anyway, my uncle didn't leave me everything," he said. "Just this property."

"Lucky you." She gazed at him with narrowed eyes, holding her empty shot glass toward him, and as he gave her a refill, he frowned a bit.

Was there a hint of larceny in her sultry stare? Or was it lust? Or, maybe the Blue Label?

Lucky you.

Sione wasn't sure if he was bothered by her comment, wasn't sure if he should read anything into it. He didn't want to think Ms. Edwards was giving him subtle provocative poses and smoldering glances because she was interested in the real estate he'd inherited from his uncle.

If she was drunk, then he wanted her to be intoxicated by the aged scotch, not the idea of scamming landholdings from him. Not that he believed she wanted to steal his property. According to his cousin, Ms. Edwards was most likely involved in white-collar shenanigans.

"Nice that your uncle cared so much about you," she said and then tossed back the scotch.

Sione wondered about her tone. He didn't think it was jealousy, more like a wishful longing. Maybe she didn't have anyone who cared about her? He didn't know and didn't think he could conclude anything. He didn't know enough about her situation, and he was probably half-drunk himself.

"It's just difficult." He put the Blue Label on the coffee table and then sat on the couch next to her, not too close but not too far away.

She looked at him, turning her body at an angle toward him, distracting him a little.

"You're thankful." He went on, staring at the empty shot glass. "But I have all the property I have because he's gone, and I appreciate it, I know it's a blessing, but ..."

"You would rather have your uncle," she said. "I know what you mean."

He glanced at her and saw the lost, forlorn look in her brown eyes. "You lost someone close to you?"

Nodding, Ms. Edwards said, "My mother."

"I'm sorry."

"I was seven." She put the shot glass on the coffee table and then leaned back against the couch cushions.

"That must have been tough."

"Brutal." She sighed. "You know, when you're young, you don't understand why bad things happen. Part of me blamed her and even hated her for leaving me."

"Death is hard when you're a kid."

Ms. Edwards turned her head toward him, a strange look on her face, her mouth parted slightly, like maybe she wanted to say something, but didn't know how. Nodding, she looked away.

"So, you were raised by your dad?" Sione asked.

"No, thank goodness," she said, shaking her head. "My dad can barely take care of himself. I would have ended up in foster care if my father had tried to raise me."

"I know what you mean," he said.

"So, I'm guessing your dad isn't in the running for Father of the Year, either?"

"To even call him a father would be a stretch," Sione said. "A gross miscarriage of justice."

She giggled a little, reaching for the shot glass again. "A gross miscarriage of justice?"

"My cousin, Truman, is always saying that," he explained. "He's a lawyer."

Ms. Edwards looked at the half-empty shot glass and then asked, "Why aren't you close to your father?"

"Uh …" He looked away, caught off guard. "I wish I knew."

"Why don't you know?" she asked. "He wasn't around a lot when you were a kid?"

He looked away, wishing he didn't have to lie. But the relationship with Richard was too complex, too volatile, too violent. Trying to explain why he and Richard would never be father and son, despite their biological ties, would be damn near impossible, and he didn't think she would understand.

He'd have to resurrect old memories he'd buried long ago, and he wanted his past to stay in the grave. Any conversation about Richard Tuiali'i was tricky and risky. He couldn't tell the complete, unabridged truth, not unless he wanted Ms. Edwards to shrink away from him, repulsed and revolted.

He would have to skip some parts and embellish others. Trying to rewrite history was dangerous, like walking on the edge of a knife. He was bound to slip, cut himself to pieces.

"When I was sixteen, I left Belize to go and live with my uncle." Sione sighed. "My dad wasn't too happy about that, and it caused a rift between us. We just kept growing apart and then, I don't know."

Ms. Edwards cleared her throat, sat up a bit. "You have brothers or sisters?"

"Uh, yeah." He looked toward the front door. "Unfortunately."

"Unfortunately?"

Pissed at himself, he said, "I shouldn't have said that."

"Why did you?"

"When I was younger, my parents weren't getting along, and my dad was getting involved with other women. One of his girlfriends got pregnant, and I wasn't happy about that, especially since it led to my parents' divorce," he said, not sure why he was being so open with her. "Anyway, I liked being the only child, so my dad having another kid kinda pissed me off. And then his other girlfriend got pregnant, and there was another kid, and this pattern continued, and now I've got half-brothers and half-sisters that I haven't even met."

"I know what you mean," she said. "I have two half-sisters. We all have the same deadbeat dad. Anyway, I was sixteen when I found out they existed, and I wasn't thrilled to meet them."

"Are you closer to them now?"

"Very close. I wouldn't make it without them," she said, gazing at the coffee table, her eyes a bit glazed, as though she were remembering something she wanted to forget. "I'm grateful they're in my life now, but I wish I had grown up with them because …"

"Because …" he prompted, wondering why she'd trailed off.

"When I was a little girl," she started, clasping her hands together, staring down at her intertwined fingers. "I really needed them, especially when my mother …"

She stopped talking abruptly and then looked at him. There was tension in her face, a passive consternation, as though she was wrestling with some internal debate, maybe brought about by thoughts of the mother she'd lost at such a young age.

He put his shot glass down and moved a bit closer to her. "I think I understand."

She frowned, a bit of suspicion in her luminous, heavy-lidded brown gaze.

Compelled to move even closer, wanting to comfort her, he said, "You needed your sisters when your mother passed away."

15

San Ignacio, Belize
Belizean Banyan Resort - Honeymoon Casita

Kiss him.

The thought slipped into Spencer's mind, sly and sensuous and *stupid*. She couldn't just kiss him, out of the blue, with no provocation. It wouldn't make any sense. She had to do something. She had to get away from the subject of her mother, which she never should have mentioned. She didn't know why she had. Maybe she was drunk. Maybe the Blue Label had her making foolish decisions, revealing things she didn't even like to admit to herself.

And now Sione "John" Tuiali'i, the gorgeous resort owner, was waiting for her to confirm that she'd needed her sisters' support after her mother had died, but she couldn't do it. It wasn't true.

Sometimes, she wished she'd grown up with Rae and Shady, but only because her childhood had been gut-wrenchingly lonely, not because she'd lost her mom. She couldn't tell him the truth—it was difficult to explain. And so, she had to kiss him.

"Ms. Edwards," he said. "I know you probably—"

Panicked, Spencer climbed onto his lap. Seconds later, her mouth was pressed against his, a bit reluctant at first, and she hesitated, wondering if she'd made a mistake, if he would push her away.

But another second later, she felt his fingers sink between the strands of her hair, cradling her skull, and the kiss deepened as their lips parted and his tongue slid into her mouth, slowly down the length of hers, swirling languidly.

Moaning softly, Spencer wrapped her arms around his neck. Kissing the resort owner was a mistake. Ben had told her to get close, but not too close—just close enough. But she wasn't really kissing him to get close to him. The kiss had nothing to do with the favor Ben was making her do. She was kissing him to get away from the topic of her mother.

He pulled back and stared at her. "Um ... did you mean to do that?"

Breathless, Spencer shook her head, gazing at his full lips. "Not really."

"You wanna stop?" He slid his finger along her bottom lip, slowly, gently.

"I'll let you know in a minute." Spencer wrapped her arms around his shoulders, and when their mouths met again, there was no hesitation, no restraint as their tongues twirled and danced in a wild, desperate frenzy.

The kiss intensified, and for Spencer, it was as if they were kissing to save their lives. Abruptly, he lay back on the couch, pulling her with him, and the kiss continued, unbroken. They moved onto their sides, pressed against each other, and as Spencer hooked a leg over his waist, he rolled them to the right.

They tumbled over the side of the couch.

Spencer squealed, and the next moment, they were on the floor between the couch and the coffee table.

Laughing, he looked at her. "This might be a little more comfortable in the bedroom."

"The bedroom." Spencer gasped, trying to catch her breath as she raised up and moved away from him, scurrying back up onto the couch.

What the hell was her damn problem? She'd told herself not to kiss him. She'd known it would be a mistake, and now she was trying to deal with her dumb decision, trying to tame the out of control desire pulling her toward him, those lustful feelings demanding to be appeased.

"Well, I just thought." He sat up, eyes full of concern and uncertainty.

"Listen, I should, um … " Spencer stammered, jumping up from the couch. "I should probably go."

The resort owner stood. "You don't have to."

Spencer looked around the living room for her purse. "Yes, um, actually, I do."

"Ms. Edwards, we're in your casita."

"Oh, yeah. Right." Heart hammering, Spencer dropped down onto the couch, rubbing her hands over her head, gathering her hair to wind it back into the bun. "Well, then you should probably go."

"Are you sure?"

No, she wasn't sure. Or, rather, she was sure. Sure that she wanted him to stay. She jumped up, rushed to the door, and opened it. "I'm absolutely sure."

He stared at her, and she could tell he was disappointed, reluctant to leave, but she couldn't give in, no matter how much she wanted to. And she *really* wanted to give in. She wanted to grab the gorgeous, sexy resort owner and drag him into the bedroom. Pushing the thoughts away, she said, "Goodnight, *John*."

16

San Ignacio, Belize
Belizean Banyan Resort - Jaguar Cafe

"Here you are, ma'am." The waitress placed a ceramic mug filled with steaming coffee and a small cup of cream in front of Spencer.

"Thank you," Spencer said.

Seven in the morning, and the resort restaurant was bustling with tourists, excited and happy, eager to stuff themselves with carbs and protein so they could get on to the next adventure. As she poured a bit of cream into the dark liquid, she heard snatches of conversation from the tables around her. Someone had gone to the Mayan ruins, someone else had dealt with a golf cart that wouldn't start in San Pedro, and another person had seen a shark while on a snorkeling trip.

Spencer had hoped eavesdropping on other tourists would take her mind off last night, when she'd kissed Sione "John" Tuiali'i. She'd obsessed about their impromptu make-out session on the couch all night, and she was still thinking about it. She was taking care to focus more on the kiss than on the reason why she'd jumped in his lap and pressed her mouth against his—to avoid the topic of her mother, a topic she always tried to avoid. Spencer brought the mug of coffee to her lips.

When she wasn't thinking about the kiss, she was remembering the time they'd spent together, meandering through the town, enjoying the bright, blue sky and the gentle breeze wafting from the calm, blue-green waters. Her memories weren't complete without a reflection of her crazy idea to help him avoid an awkward situation with the girl he hadn't called back.

As a result of that silly attempt, Spencer now thought of him more as "John" than Sione Tuiali'i, the resort owner. She wasn't sure why, but when she thought of him as "John," he became to her more approachable, more attainable. Someone she might be able to laugh with and maybe share a few secrets. Sione Tuiali'i, the resort owner, was someone she had to get close to but not too close.

She was being forced to trick Sione Tuiali'i with seductive manipulation, and she hoped her deception would entice him to ask her out to dinner. She had to pray she was pretty enough to fool him into thinking she was worth his time and effort. She wanted to think she could get as close to "John" as she wanted. She could be vulnerable with him, and kiss him like there was no tomorrow, and she didn't have to play the part of a sexpot, trying to scam him into wanting her. "John" would think she was beautiful, but her looks wouldn't be the reason for his interest.

"Got something for you."

Jolted, Spencer looked up.

The sweaty, lecherous cab driver pulled out the chair across from her, taking a seat she hadn't offered.

"What the hell are you doing here?" Spencer put the mug on the table. "I finished the damn side ventures."

"Ain't here about the side ventures." He leered at her, swiping fingers beneath his bulbous nose. "Got something to help you with *Step Three*." The cab driver delved a hand inside his dusty, denim jacket, pulled out a small, square box, and pushed it across the table toward her.

Apprehensive, Spencer stared at the box, pulse racing, and her mind swirled with questions. Why was Ben giving her something to help her with *Step Three*? She hadn't even completed *Step Two*. She was still working on getting John to invite her to dinner and back to his casita.

"What is this?"

"Mr. Chang will contact you," he said, his words like a threat.

"When?" she asked.

Saying nothing, the cab driver got up from the table, turned his back to her, and lumbered away. Spencer stared at the small box again, reluctant to touch it, let alone open it and find out what was inside. She didn't want to know, but she forced herself to lift the lid.

Seconds later, Spencer stared at the contents, trembling, feeling as though a bomb had gone off inside her, rocking her to her very foundations. She didn't want to believe what she saw. She knew what it meant, and she knew why Ben had sent it to her. Taking a deep breath, Spencer tried not to scream.

17

Pacing across the bedroom in her casita, Spencer pressed the burner phone to her ear, spewing a string of vicious curses at Ben.

"You damn liar, you said I wouldn't have to do anything criminal!"

An hour had passed since she'd received Ben's little box from the sweaty cab driver. Something to help her with *Step Three*. Spencer wasn't sure how long she'd sat at the table, paralyzed, but eventually, she'd managed to compose herself enough to pay her bill, stand up, and walk out of the restaurant without collapsing.

Once she'd seen what was inside the small, square box, she'd known Ben had lied to her. And she wasn't surprised. All his promises about not making her do anything criminal had been bullshit! Bastard! Always making snide remarks about her leaving him to die on the floor. Right now, she wished he had died. She wished she had plunged that knife into his heart.

"Sweet girl, please calm down," Ben said, his tone patronizing. "Let me explain what I need you to do."

"I know what you want me to do!" She paced to the wardrobe, then turned, and stomped toward the dresser. "You want me to drug the resort owner and steal something from him!"

Even now, her heart almost stopped when she remembered how shocked she'd been after she opened the box and saw the small vial of liquid. She'd known it could only be one thing. The elixir of oblivion, as Rae liked to refer to it. GHB.

"Don't get ahead of yourself, sweet girl," Ben said. "Don't assume that you know what I want you to do."

"I'm not going to drug Sione," Spencer said, pacing toward the foot of the bed. "So forget about me pouring the contents of that vial into his wine."

"Sweet girl, don't tell me what you're not going to do," Ben said. "I will tell you what you are going to do, understand?"

Weary and remorseful, Spencer sank down on the bed, hands trembling as she held the phone to her ear, listening.

"And once I tell you," he said. "I will accept no argument, I will entertain no alternatives from you, do you understand?"

"Yeah," she said, squeezing her eyes shut, willing herself not to cry. "I understand."

"Now, listen carefully," he said. "The GHB is for *Step Three*. But you will not receive instructions for *Step Three* until you complete *Step Two*, which, to date, you have not done."

"I'm working on it."

"I believe you are, sweet girl. You certainly seemed to be working on it when Sione accompanied you on the last side venture in San Pedro," Ben said. "The two of you seemed very close as you strolled along the beach."

"We weren't as close as we seemed," she snipped, disturbed but not surprised he'd been watching her.

"That was clever, sweet girl, but risky," Ben said.

"Don't worry, he has no clue why I was really there," Spencer said.

"Well, I'm not surprised. Tricking men is your specialty."

Spencer rolled her eyes at his insult.

Ben continued, "So, I'm sure you'll get him to ask you to dinner. Once that happens, and it should happen sooner rather than later, call me, and I'll have further instructions for you."

18

"Tell me this," D.J. said, closing the door behind him after he walked into Sione's office. "Why the hell did you go to San Pedro with Spencer Edwards without telling me? I'm supposed to be following her, remember? I'm supposed to be trying to find out what the hell she's up to."

Leaning back in his chair, Sione asked, "How do you know I went to San Pedro with her?"

"Your whole staff is talking about it," D.J. said.

Sione sighed and asked, "What are they saying?"

"Ask Marie," D.J. said. "Now, tell me what happened in San Pedro."

"Relax, okay," Sione said. "She didn't do anything suspicious."

"Are you sure?" D.J. walked to the chair in front of the desk and took a seat.

Sione shrugged. "She just went shopping. She didn't swap bags with anybody either. She took a white beach bag to San Pedro, and she had the same white beach bag with her when we came back to the resort."

"And then what happened?"

"What do you mean?"

"You know what I mean," D.J. said, scowling. "What happened when you went back to the honeymoon casita with her?"

"Don't tell me." Sione shook his head. "The staff is talking about that, too?"

Nodding, D.J. said, "So, what happened."

Sione shrugged. "Nothing much."

That perturbed him, especially when he remembered walking into her dressing room at the boutique and finding her half-dressed. Her body was luscious and exquisite, just as he'd imagined it would be beneath the skimpy, clingy clothes she wore.

"Nothing much?" D.J. gave him a skeptical frown. "You expect me to believe that you were alone with a gorgeous, sexy girl like her and nothing much happened."

"Believe it or not, but we just talked," he said, ignoring his cousin's dubious looks.

He wasn't about to tell D.J. that Ms. Edwards had kicked him out after she had jumped on his lap and kissed him. He wasn't about to tell him how he'd stood on the porch in the dark, still hard as a brick, feeling like a fool, confused and wondering what the hell he had done wrong. He certainly was not going to tell his cousin the kiss had kept him up most of the night, and even now, he couldn't stop thinking about how soft her lips felt and couldn't stop wishing they had gone further.

D.J. would never let him hear the end of it.

"You know, she might have changed her M.O.," D.J. said.

"What do you mean?"

"Maybe she did make a delivery on the San Pedro trip," D.J. said. "But maybe it didn't involve switching bags this time. Maybe she took something out of her bag and left it somewhere, or passed it to someone, when you weren't looking?"

Shaking his head, Sione said, "I don't think so."

He wasn't really sure, though. When he and Ms. Edwards had traveled to San Pedro, he hadn't been skeptical of her motives, wondering if she was planning another delivery. She'd looked so beautiful in the sun-drenched setting of powdery white sand, clear turquoise water, and swaying palm trees in the gentle breeze. He found himself enjoying her company. He hadn't been looking for suspicious activity.

"Well, here's something you might find interesting," D.J. said. "Yesterday morning, Ms. Edwards had breakfast at the Jaguar Café. About fifteen minutes after she was seated, she was joined by some guy. Sloppy dude, mid-forties, maybe. Soft around the middle, sweaty."

Sione sat forward. "That's not the guy who broke into her casita."

"Guy wasn't Asian," D.J. confirmed. "And didn't have a snake tattoo on his face."

"Who do you think the sloppy guy is?"

"Not sure," D.J. said. "Maybe her partner. Maybe a contact here in San Ignacio. He gave her a gift. A little box, like the kind you'd put jewelry in. Don't think she liked what she got."

"Why not?"

"Probably wasn't enough carats." His cousin smirked. "She probably doesn't spread those legs for anything less than ten—"

"David ..."

D.J. said, "When she opened the box, the look on her face was ..."

"Was what?"

"Fear," his cousin said. "She looked really afraid."

Worried, Sione asked, "Afraid that the guy was going to hurt her or something?"

"I don't know. Maybe. Anyway," D.J. went on. "I followed the guy to a house in Bullet Tree Village. The place is owned by a company called The Leviathan Group. But I was able to find out that it's being rented by William Bermudez. He's got a record, but nothing dangerous. Arrested for trying to use a stolen credit card. Got probation. Nevertheless, I saw his mug shot and got confirmation that he's the guy who had breakfast with Ms. Edwards. So maybe I'll have a talk with him. Maybe he'll rat her out."

"Assuming there's something to rat on her about," Sione said. "Because maybe there's not. Maybe she's innocent. Maybe there's a logical explanation for why the passports and the money was delivered to her."

D.J. gave him a look.

Sione frowned. "What?"

"You like Ms. Edwards, don't you?"

"I like Ms. Edwards?" Sione bristled. "What the hell? Are we in the fourth grade? I *like* Ms. Edwards?"

Shoulders shaking, D.J. chuckled and shook his head.

"What the hell is so funny?"

"Actually, it's not funny," D.J. said and then let out a deep sigh as his laughter subsided. "You remember I asked you if you'd have a problem dealing with the truth about Ms. Edwards?"

"I guess."

"Reason I asked you is because I could tell you might catch feelings for this woman."

"Catch feelings?" Sione sat back, glaring at his cousin. "Be serious."

"I am serious," D.J. said. "If I thought this was just one of those hit-it-and-forget-it situations, I wouldn't say anything. But I can tell you don't like the idea of this woman being a lying con artist."

"I don't," Sione said. "But not for whatever reason you're thinking. I don't want her pulling some scam at my resort."

"Dude, listen to me. You don't want to get involved with this woman," D.J. said. "I can already tell she's flawless danger."

Confused, Sione stared at his cousin. "Flawless danger?"

"Beautiful but deadly," D.J. explained, dropping his voice to imitate the tone and exaggerated inflection of an action suspense movie trailer. "Her face is flawless but all she brings to your life is danger."

"Shut the hell up." Sione grabbed a sheet of paper he didn't need, balled it up, and then hurled it at D.J., who deftly blocked it with his wrist.

Chuckling again, D.J. said, "I needed a good laugh."

"I'm glad you could have it at my expense," Sione said, debating whether to ask his cousin why he needed a laugh.

He decided he wouldn't shake the tree. No telling what might fall down and knock him over the head. Besides, he had enough issues of his own. He would stay out of his cousin's marital woes.

"You know I'm right," D.J. went on. "You like those girls, they look good, but they are bad for you. They always wind up in trouble, and then you always run to the rescue because you are Captain Save-A-Ho and that's what you do."

"Are you finished?" Sione asked. "Because the way I see it, we still don't know what's going on with Ms. Edwards."

"Maybe we don't," D.J. conceded. "But there is something I do know."

"What's that?" Sione asked, distracted by thoughts of his family's perception of him. Captain Save-A-Ho. Might have been insulting if it was true, but it wasn't.

Sione was far from a hero. His family didn't know he'd been raised to be the villain, and they never would.

"I found out who came to see Moana before she was killed."

Sione's pulse jumped, and he grabbed a stack of papers to straighten. He'd asked D.J. for a list of Moana's visitors, but he realized he'd been hoping D.J. wouldn't be able to find out anything. Now that his cousin had the answers, Sione wasn't so sure he wanted to know.

D.J. cleared his throat and then said, "Besides her attorney, some chick named Kelsey Thomas went to see her."

"Kelsey Thomas?" Sione stared at his cousin, not sure he'd heard him right. Kelsey Thomas had visited Moana? What the hell was that about? How did Kelsey Thomas know Moana?

"You know her?" D.J. asked.

"Don't think so," Sione lied, trying to get over the shock.

D.J. said, "Well, another visitor is someone you won't believe."

"Someone I won't believe?"

"Peter."

Sione frowned. "Peter? Wait, Peter Rios? *Our cousin* Peter? That Peter?"

"That Peter," D.J. confirmed.

"Why the hell would Peter go to visit Moana?"

"Maybe you should ask him."

Sitting back in his chair, Sione rubbed his jaw. Why would Peter go to visit Moana? They knew each other, and Peter had always had a quasi-crush on Moana, so it wasn't out of the realm of possibility. But it was definitely out of the realm of *probability*.

"She had another interesting visitor," D.J. said.

Sione glanced at D.J., trying to stay calm, trying to ignore the strange twitch he felt beneath the surface of his skin. "Who?"

"Your father went to see Moana," D.J. said.

Sione leaned forward, resting his elbows on the desk, trying to come to terms with the truth. There was no more suspicion, no more speculation. Moana hadn't lied to him, but Sione cautioned himself not to jump to the conclusions she'd tried to convince him to believe. Richard had visited her, and that was true. But had his father threatened her life when he'd gone to see her in prison?

Moana had been a deceitful bitch, Sione had to remember that. She'd been desperate to get out of prison, and she wouldn't have been above exploiting the issues between him and his father to her advantage. The conversation between Richard and Moana might have been very different from what she'd told him.

"Do you know what that was about?" D.J. asked. "Why would Richard visit her? Thought he hated her? Thought he blamed her for the beef between you and Ben."

"He does hate her," Sione said. "That's why it makes no sense that he would visit her."

"Are you going to find out why your father went to see her?"

"He probably wouldn't tell me the truth," Sione said.

He wasn't sure if he wanted to know the truth. Had Richard threatened Moana? Had his father arranged to have his ex-fiancée killed? The answers to those questions would be a burden, and Sione wasn't sure he wanted to bear it.

19

San Ignacio, Belize

Belizean Banyan Resort - Honeymoon Casita

Around eight the next morning, Spencer walked into the bathroom, stripping as she headed for the shower. In her head was a whimsical little tune, something John's little cousins had been singing when they tried to show her how to do a samba. The trio of little sprites were so cute, and thinking about them made her think of herself at their age, around six or seven years old. When life was carefree and she didn't have to worry about the consequences of her stupid decisions and foolish mistakes. Well, she supposed things weren't exactly carefree when she was seven.

There had been times when she didn't have to worry, mostly during the summer months, when she was shipped off to live with her grandparents. Back then, every day was spent with her favorite cousins, Rusty and Jennifer, getting into "devilment," as her grandfather called their playful mischief, making mud pies, "playing school," and just being wild and happy and free.

Of course, at the end of summer, there were always bitter tears. She'd sobbed because she had to go back home, back to her mother, back to staying as quiet as possible, back to wondering if she would go to bed hungry, and back to the fear of being kicked and scratched and then left alone to fend for herself—just her and her tears and the pain of wounds, both emotional and physical, that never seemed to heal.

Standing beneath the showerhead, Spencer allowed the hot water to wash away the sadness of her childhood, and as she lathered the honey-and-lavender soap over her skin, she forced herself to remember the fun she'd had with John's little second cousins. All the laughter and the games had made her feel content, settled, and she'd enjoyed it.

With no children of her own, Spencer had always figured she wouldn't know what to do with herself around kids. She always thought she'd be uncomfortable and stiff. She actually liked playing with the girls. They were a surprising amusement. And yet, it was bittersweet. She'd started to wonder what it might be like to have a family of her own and children to love and spoil, ridiculous fantasies she couldn't afford to indulge in.

Spencer turned the water off, stepped out of the shower, and grabbed a towel. Back in the bedroom, she opened the top dresser drawer and pulled out a bra and panties. Laughing a little, she smiled to herself and remembered how the little girls had left John exhausted. She put on the bra and underwear.

John would probably make a good father to three little fairies of his own one day. The thought made her pause and gave her conflicting emotions she didn't want to acknowledge or deal with. It would mean he'd found someone to be Mrs. Tuiali'i.

Some very lucky woman who wouldn't be her. The thought bothered her, though it shouldn't have. Spencer didn't even want to get married. If there was ever a man who could turn her into "that wife,", it was probably Sione "John" Tuiali'i. She could imagine herself very submissive in his presence, following all of his dictates, no matter how degrading or debilitating.

The phone rang. Confused by the ringing, it took Spencer a few moments to realize it wasn't her cell phone and it wasn't—thank God —the burner phone Ben had given her. It was the casita phone on the bed table.

Spencer went to answer it, wondering who the hell could be calling. The front desk, maybe? Probably the idiot desk assistant, Analee, calling to deliver a wake-up call Spencer hadn't requested.

"Hello?"

"Spencer?" A terse, tense female voice said. "It's Maxine Porter."

Puzzled, Spencer sat on the edge of the bed. "Maxine Porter?"

"You delivered the prescription medication to me a few days ago?"

"Oh, yeah, right," Spencer said, her stomach twisting with a twinge of dread. "Hi, how are you?"

"I need to see you," Maxine said. "Today. This morning. It's really important."

"Why do you need to see me?"

"We have a problem," Maxine said.

"What kind of problem?"

"Not over the phone," Maxine said, her tone clipped and curt. "I need to see you in person."

Annoyed, Spencer said, "Listen, I don't have time to—"

"No, you listen," Maxine said. "If you want to leave Belize alive, then you need to meet me."

Pulse racing, Spencer sank down on the bed, not sure how to respond. The woman was being melodramatic, probably trying to scare her. Spencer wanted to tell her to go to hell and then slam the phone down. Maybe that wasn't a good idea, though. Maybe she needed to find out about this problem because she absolutely wanted to leave Belize alive.

Finally, Spencer said, "Okay, fine. Where do you want me to meet you? At the boutique?"

"I'm not working today," Maxine said. "You can come to my place."

"Your place?" Dozens of clanging warning bells went off within Spencer. "Why can't we meet in public?"

"We can't talk about this in public," Maxine said.

Trying to ignore the internal warnings, Spencer said, "Fine. Give me your address."

20

San Ignacio, Belize

Belizean Banyan Resort - Owner's Office

Sitting in his office, Sione stared at the employment applications he'd received for the Pool Assistant position. He'd planned to spend the morning reviewing resumes, but he couldn't focus. For the past few days, he hadn't been able to stop thinking about Moana's death and the role his father might have played in it. The situation with Ms. Edwards consumed his thoughts as well. Sione wasn't convinced she was running a scam, but he wasn't sure she was clueless and innocent either.

Feeling the need to make some sort of judgment on the situation, Sione wanted to clarify his position. But he wasn't sure of the best way to do that. Should his opinion be based on gut instinct or logic? A rational approach would be best, he decided, based on facts, not wild speculation.

Abandoning the employment applications, Sione opened the pencil drawer, looking for the blue folder D.J. had given him. The file contained the printed version of the PowerPoint presentation including all the photos his cousin had snapped of Ms. Edwards. Photographic evidence of … Sione wasn't sure what. Not necessarily a crime being committed, but definitely something suspicious.

After a few minutes, he gave up the search, remembering that the blue folder was in his casita office. Sione leaned back in his chair, a bit disappointed. The photos would jog his memory and help nail down the facts, but that wasn't the only reason he'd wanted to look at them. He'd really just wanted a legitimate excuse to enjoy several photos of a good-looking woman. Because the photos had been taken without her consent, Sione felt a little weird looking at them simply for personal enjoyment.

Even without the pictures, he was aware of the facts. But from those facts, what could be deduced? Nothing definitive. Only speculation.

He wasn't even sure what had been inside those beach bags Ms. Edwards had taken on her excursions to the Mayan ruins and the cave tour. He couldn't assume she'd stuffed the bags with the Xanax boxes filled with fake passports and money. There was no proof to support D.J.'s assumptions she was involved in something criminal.

Marie buzzed. "D.J. is on two."

Sione grabbed the phone. "What's going on?"

"Ms. Edwards is leaving the resort," D.J. said. "I have it on good authority—said authority being Analee, who agreed to give me a heads-up about Ms. Edwards' comings and goings—that she called for a cab and asked about a ferry to San Pedro."

"You going to follow her?"

"That's why I called you," D.J. said and then exhaled. "I have a call I have to take, so I was hoping you could get things started, and I'll pick up the slack as soon as I can."

Sione gripped the phone. "You think she's going to make another delivery?"

"Maybe. I'm not sure," D.J. said. "But, if so, one of us needs to be there. So don't lose her. And do not let her catch you following her."

21

Clutching her stomach, Spencer swallowed, praying she wouldn't get sick as the water taxi sped through the Caribbean, hitting waves and jostling her up and down and side to side. The motor was a buzzing roar, making it nearly impossible to think.

Impossible to figure out what Maxine had meant when she'd said we have a problem. What the hell kind of problem? With the money, maybe? Maybe Maxine Porter hadn't received the correct amount of money she'd been promised.

Spencer thought back to the freckle-faced tomboy who'd held a gun on her.

Had Maxine counted her money and realized she'd been shorted?

Salty sea spray came into the open-air boat, teaming with the wind to make a mess of the chignon she'd barely been able to twist her hair into. Shivering, Spencer reached into her purse and grabbed the slip of paper she'd written Maxine Porter's address on.

Estrella Estates. #309. A condo on the far northern end of Ambergris Caye, the woman had told her.

Staring at the foamy wake of the boat, Spencer wondered if maybe there was a problem with the passport. Or maybe the problem was with Ben? Or maybe it was something worse than she could imagine.

If you want to leave Belize alive.

Clasping her hands together, Spencer looked down at the canvas shoes she'd chosen to wear, along with khaki shorts and a camouflage print tank. She had a habit of dressing for her audience, which tended to be men, old jackasses who liked curves and lots of unabashed cleavage. Meeting a woman she hardly knew to deal with a situation she hardly understood didn't require her usual clingy dresses and heels.

Although, a six-inch stiletto might come in handy if Maxine got belligerent and tried to start a physical altercation.

As the shoreline of Ambergris Caye came into view, Spencer stared at the beach and the palm trees swaying in the breeze, remembering the day she and John had gone to San Pedro. She would never admit it, but as they'd walked along the beach, she'd felt like a new bride with her husband, and she'd wondered if any of the other tourists staring at them had come to the same conclusion. Secretly, for some reason, she hoped they had.

Foolish thoughts, Spencer knew. But why? Was she starting to like the idea of getting too close to the resort owner?

Each time she talked to her sisters, they never failed to question her interest in John. Usually, Spencer ignored their blatant insinuations or dodged and evaded their inquiries. She was afraid of the answer, afraid she might be interested in the resort owner. As the ferry pulled over to the dock, she forced herself to forget about John. Right now, she had to deal with Maxine Porter.

22

San Pedro, Belize
Ambergris Caye

As soon as the captain steered the water taxi to the edge of the pier, Sione was on his feet, climbing out of the boat.

Passengers were still unloading from the ferry docked in front of the water taxi. One of them was Ms. Edwards, who allowed a smiling deckhand to offer her assistance as she made her way down a set of portable plastic steps and onto the wooden pier. As she headed toward the end of the dock, the deckhands watched her walk away, no doubt glad to see her go.

Walking along the weather-beaten planks, Sione made sure to keep Ms. Edwards in sight and enjoyed the view, as well. She was dressed in shorts, a camouflage sleeveless tank top, and canvas shoes, yet she still managed to look extra sexy. Sione was used to seeing her in body-defining dresses with dangerous plunging necklines, and he wondered if there was some specific reason for the casual attire. Was she anticipating a situation where she might have to get away quick or run for her life? Sione hoped not, but if the circumstances went sideways, he wasn't going to let anything bad happen to her.

He was still upset about the Asian guy who'd broken into the honeymoon casita and attacked her. When he'd seen the bastard on top of Ms. Edwards, trying to tie her hands behind her back, Sione had wanted to tear something apart.

He'd felt a familiar instinct growing within him, the anger that went beyond indignation, the rage that went too far, demanding a violent reaction, a need to both defend and avenge. Sione had fought to keep the anger in check. He'd tried to remember he wasn't that person anymore. He didn't have to indulge in the anger and let the negative emotions control him, or dictate his actions, the way he'd been taught to do. But he'd never been the type to just sit on his ass and do nothing. The bruised knuckles hadn't exactly been appreciated, but he didn't feel too bad about beating the crap out of some son of a bitch who clearly deserved it.

As Sione made his way onto the beach, following a cluster of elderly tourists, he donned a baseball cap and sunglasses, trying to disguise himself. Ms. Edwards still might recognize him if she decided to look over her shoulder. Better keep a bit of distance between them, he decided. Maybe ten to fifteen feet.

Sione weaved through tourists and then stopped between two palm trees as Ms. Edwards walked down a narrow alley between a restaurant and a hotel. She was headed west, toward Front Street. He figured the main road through San Pedro would be her destination.

Scanning the alley, he realized there weren't enough people traversing the narrow passageway to follow directly behind her. If she turned, there would be no crowd where he could blend into or get lost in. Taking a chance, he decided to take a different route to Front Street, confident he would spot her once he got to the main road.

Angling toward a beachfront hotel, he took the stairs two at a time and then followed the veranda around to the back of the hotel, where stairs led down to Front Street. Even at ten in the morning, the main drag was cluttered and clogged with tourists, locals, and listless dogs, meandering aimlessly along the road.

D.J. had told him not to lose her, but Sione figured it would be impossible to lose sight of Ms. Edwards, even if he allowed her to get even farther ahead. And he was right. Those curves were like a tracking device, and he followed her sexy sway as she crossed the road and stepped up onto the sidewalk.

Walking along the opposite side of Front Street, he kept his focus on Ms. Edwards as she passed several storefronts and shops, her pace brisk as she moved in and out of the ebb and flow of human traffic.

As a group of four or five girls in short dresses and heels sauntered toward him, laughing and giggling, Sione stepped between two parked golf carts, allowing them to pass.

Across the street, Ms. Edwards struggled to make her way through a large group of European tourists, and at one point, Sione lost sight of her, but then he found her again as she squeezed through two round, ruddy-faced grandmotherly types.

A pick-up truck rumbled down the street, and after it passed, Sione searched for Ms. Edwards among the tourists, but couldn't pick her out.

One of the girls stared openly at Sione as the five of them passed him, and then she whispered something to her friends who looked over as they walked along, still giggling, and he forced himself to look pleasant because he couldn't manage a smile.

The tourists had crowded into a souvenir shop, but he didn't see Ms. Edwards. Where the hell had she gone? Cursing, he picked up his pace, threading through the tourists as he scanned the opposite side of the street. He was about to cross the road when he saw Ms.

Edwards standing in front of a bar about a quarter mile down the road. Seconds later, a blue cab pulled over to the curb and Ms. Edwards got in. *Damn!*

The blue cab rolled away from the curb, heading south down Front Street. His heart pounding, Sione turned. Through the back windshield, he saw Ms. Edwards sitting in the cab, heading away from him.

Rushing down the street, he spotted a row of golf carts parked in front of a restaurant. Using the cover of excited, distracted tourists and the nonchalance of the locals, he walked between the golf carts, scanning ignition switches, hoping to find a cart with the key still inside.

Peripherally, he saw a cab heading south. Abandoning his search for a golf cart to steal, he stepped out into the street and stopped, preventing the cab from continuing down the road.

The driver leaned out of the window. "Get out of the way! I almost hit you!"

"I need you to follow that cab," Sione said, taking out his wallet and ignoring the honking horns of the cars lined up behind the cab he'd stopped in the middle of the street.

"What you talking about?" The driver frowned at him. "You crazy?"

Walking to the driver's window, Sione dropped a one-hundred-dollar bill on the driver's lap, opened the rear door, and got in.

23

Spencer closed her eyes as the cab jostled over paved stones.

Despite the low clouds promising more thundershowers, San Pedro was full of life, bursting at the seams with music and bright beckoning lights, an invitation to a shot of bacchanal glee. People were having a good time, laughing and talking, stepping to the beat of a lively harmony wafting along on the tail of the wind.

With the rear windows rolled down, Spencer thought it would be impossible to drown out the passing revelry, but nothing could drown out the sound of her heart punching against her ribcage. She didn't know what to think about the situation with Maxine Porter. What could the damn problem be? And why did she have to be involved in coming up with a solution?

She should have known the side venture would be problematic despite Ben's promise that nothing would go wrong if she followed his instructions. Well, she'd done exactly what he'd told her to do. And what had obedience gotten her?

Why was she surprised? She was used to dealing with problems and obstacles. Anything she'd ever had to endure had always been painstaking and laborious, depleting her emotionally, physically, and spiritually.

Rubbing her eyes, Spencer told herself to cancel the pity party and focus. This problem with Maxine had the potential to become a huge mess. She needed to think of some way out of the mess before she became stuck in it. Without knowing what the problem was, it was difficult to figure out what sort of defense she needed. She had to think of something because she suspected the situation might blow up in her face, leaving her shell-shocked and damaged beyond repair.

"Ma'am, here you are." The driver's voice was jarring, like a slap.

Slowly, Spencer opened her eyes and became aware of her surroundings. The cab had stopped along a deserted stretch of unpaved road. Across the street, an expansive complex of Spanish-style condos with red-tiled roofs loomed toward wispy clouds smeared across the hazy, faded gray sky.

Spencer hesitated. She didn't want to get out. She wanted to tell the driver to turn around and take her back to Front Street so she could get on the next ferry and get back to the resort. The drive over the bumpy, unpaved road had jostled not just her bones but also her nerves, leaving her agitated and paranoid. Coming here was a mistake. Maybe even some kind of setup. Spencer had a feeling Maxine was trying to pull something, but what?

"Ma'am," the cab driver prompted.

"Um, sorry." Spencer took a deep breath. "How much do I owe you?"

24

———————

San Pedro, Belize
Estrella Estates

Trying to stay calm and not think the worst, Sione exhaled a deep breath as the driver tried his best to avoid a series of potholes.

The blue cab had first taken Ms. Edwards about a mile or so out of town and was now maneuvering down a stretch of road, which hadn't been paved yet. Sione felt every bump, rut, and pothole along the nearly deserted road, and each time the chassis jostled and shook, he felt disgruntled and angry.

He was pissed at himself for losing sight of Ms. Edwards on Front Street. He'd only looked away for a few minutes, but those few minutes had been enough time for her to get in a cab and head away from town. Thank God, he'd been able to get a cab moments later, while Ms. Edwards' cab was still in sight.

But what if he hadn't been able to get a cab? Or what if he had but only after the blue cab had turned off Front Street? He wouldn't have known which way she'd instructed the driver to go.

Sione didn't want to think about her alone in San Pedro heading into God only knew what, with no protection, no one to watch her back. He didn't want to think about anything preventing him from making sure nothing bad happened to Ms. Edwards. But why? He didn't understand why he felt so protective toward her. He didn't really even know her or anything about her like whether she was working some scam or not, though it was starting to look that way.

All the evidence pointed to her working some con. The money and fake passports hidden in those Xanax boxes. The Mayan ruins tour where she appeared to have left a bag behind for another tourist to take. The cave exploration trip where she had switched bags with another tourist. And today, this second excursion to San Pedro, which made him wonder if the first trip hadn't really been for retail therapy but maybe reconnaissance.

But all the evidence was circumstantial. Until there was concrete proof against her, he wasn't going to get the police involved.

"He's letting her out," the driver said, slowing for a stop sign at the corner of the street the blue cab had just turned onto. "What do you want me to do?"

Sione turned toward the rear passenger window and scanned the road. Ms. Edwards got out of the cab and closed the door. After walking around the back of the blue cab, she hurried across the street, toward a large complex of three-story condominiums designed in the style of Spanish villas with stucco exterior and red-tiled roofs.

"I see why you wanted to follow her," the driver said and then let out a lusty cackle along with a few lewd words in Spanish.

Sione wanted to crack him in the jaw, but he ignored the innuendo and kept his gaze on Spencer as she walked toward a small parking lot. His viewpoint was limited by the angle of the cab and the cluster of trees along the fence line of the lot. No sooner had Ms. Edwards stepped foot on the gravel surface than she disappeared behind the dense, low-hanging foliage surrounding the area.

Sione opened the door. "I'll get out here."

25

Skirting puddles, Spencer headed toward the condos where Maxine lived. Taking more deep breaths, she tried not to panic as she walked along the edge of the road, several feet from bushes and low brush growing wild and haphazardly.

The sprawling complex was called Estrella Estates, and despite the dense, gray clouds and damp, humid atmosphere, it looked impressive, exclusive, and expensive—not the sort of place you could afford on a store clerk's salary.

A few yards ahead, ten-foot wrought-iron gates announced the entrance to the complex, but Maxine had told her to bypass the main entrance. Following the woman's instructions, Spencer hurried across a palm-shaded parking lot, passing several golf carts, one car, and a few bicycles leaning against the trunk of a large allspice tree.

Ahead, she saw the laundry building Maxine had told her to pass through. At the door, she twisted the knob. Hinges squeaked as she pushed the door open. Cloistered heat and the scent of fabric softener hit her in the face. Several dryers were going, clothes tumbling in circles, and a washer was on the spin cycle. Spencer hurried to the opposite side of the room, toward the door Maxine had said would open out to the grounds of the complex.

Her heart sank a bit when the door opened easily. Secretly, Spencer had hoped the door would be locked. A locked door would have given her an excuse not to meet with Maxine. She couldn't stop thinking about the last thing Maxine had told her.

If you want to leave Belize alive.

What was Maxine trying to make her think? If the problem wasn't handled, Spencer might end up dead? And, if so, who would kill her? Ben? Spencer didn't think so. He'd had so many chances to hurt her, and he'd blown every opportunity to kill her. Spencer couldn't risk it though. What was that old saying? The straw that broke the camel's back? If the problem was that some of Maxine's money was missing and Ben thought she'd stolen the money, he might go over the edge and into a rage—against her.

Spencer made her way through the maze of pathways, searching for unit 309. Now and then, the sun peeked through the clouds, a thin ray of light winking through the gloom. Sun usually made her feel more hopeful. Spencer wanted the hint of sunlight to encourage her and convince her that things would be okay, but it was impossible. With each step, her paranoia and apprehension increased. She was afraid the dense, heavy clouds were a sign that things would turn out to be much worse than she could have ever imagined.

26

Stopping near an allspice tree along the fence line of the condominium complex, Sione stayed in the shadows as Ms. Edwards headed into a small building at the far end of the gravel surface lot.

Why was she at the Estrella Estates? How did she know about this place? Who had told her to come here? The sloppy guy D.J. had seen talking to her at the Jaguar Café maybe? Was he her partner?

Sione hurried across the gravel lot to the small building. Taking a chance, he opened the door. It was empty except for washers and dryers humming and spinning—a laundry room. Assuming Spencer had exited through a second door on the opposite side of the room, near a row of washing machines, he did likewise. Back outside, he realized she'd bypassed the main entrance and taken a shortcut to get onto the complex grounds.

Ahead, Ms. Edwards rounded the corner of a building, and he lost sight of her. Cursing, Sione picked up his pace. He went around the corner of the building. She wasn't there. Cursing again, he followed the path to the end, where it forked in three directions. D.J.'s warning echoed in his head. *Don't lose her.* Sione would never hear the end of it from his cousin if he managed to let Ms. Edwards give him the slip. Sione looked right and saw nothing but an empty path curving though the buildings. Trying not to panic, he turned left. There she was. Relieved, he resumed following her, telling himself to stay focused.

As she walked, Sione had to stop himself from calling out to her. D.J. had warned him not to let her catch him following her. But Sione didn't want to follow her. He didn't like stalking her. It bothered him that she had no idea he was tailing her, watching her every move.

He wanted to come clean with her. He wanted to tell her he knew about the money and passports and then offer to help her out of whatever situation she was trapped in. Sione had a feeling she was in over her head, but she didn't know it, and by the time she figured it out, it might be too late.

Sione saw her head down a path toward a corner unit, and he slipped behind a cluster of A/C units surrounded by oleander trees. He peeked between the flowering leaves. Ms. Edwards stood at the gate of unit 309. Sione waited and watched.

27

———————

"Maxine?" Spencer called out, tapping on the gate. "Are you here? It's Spencer Edwards. You called me and said you wanted to see me. You said it was important. Are you in here?"

Her heart slamming, Spencer stood in front of the wooden gate to unit 309, a ground floor corner unit shrouded by large hibiscus trees. Pulling the gate open, Spencer stepped onto the enclosed porch. The front door was open, and the screen door was closed.

Spencer walked to the screen door, cupped her hands against the glass, and peered inside. The interior was shrouded in shadows, but she could see the condo had an open layout. The kitchen was a few feet from the door and gave way to a dining area and then the living room at the far end.

"Maxine ..."

She glanced over her shoulder at the stucco wall and then back at the screen door. Maybe Maxine had stepped out to get her mail. Maybe she was in the bathroom? Maybe she was out on the patio? Or maybe this was a mistake. She shouldn't have come here. And she should probably leave.

"Maxine?" Spencer grabbed the handle of the screen door, deciding to yank on it, hoping the racket would alert Maxine to her presence. "Max—"

The door flew open toward her. Startled, Spencer gasped and stepped back but then grabbed the door so it wouldn't slam against the frame. Using an arm to hold the screen door open, she stared into the condo, her frustration slipping away as the apprehension returned. Wary, she entered the condo.

It was dim inside but the patio, near the living room, allowed a bit of light to filter in through slightly opened vertical blinds. Spencer didn't understand. Why would Maxine call her, demand to see her, stress the importance of needing to meet to discuss the problem, and then not be at home? Where the hell was she?

Spencer approached the dining area, walking past a table that seated six. Exhaling a shaky breath, Spencer thought maybe she should just leave. Obviously, Maxine wasn't there. Why? Who knew? And Spencer didn't care. She was out of there.

Halfway to the door, she stopped, thinking that maybe she should leave a note. Something short and sour. *I showed up. You weren't here. I left.* She could leave her number for Maxine, with a request to call her. And maybe she could get Maxine's number.

Using Maxine's phone, Spencer could call her own cell phone so Maxine's house number would be displayed on the cell phone caller ID. When Spencer got back to the resort, she could call Maxine from her cell phone. Maybe the woman would be home by then and they could figure out how the hell they'd missed each other.

In the living room, she looked for a pen and paper. After scanning the coffee and end tables and a low bookshelf behind the loveseat, she found nothing.

Spencer glanced over her shoulder again.

The screen door beckoned, begging her to turn and run out of it, but she tried to ignore the strange, sudden panic slicing through her. She needed to find a pen and something to scribble a message across. She'd have to check the bedroom. Maybe there was a study. Walking through an opening in the wall, she headed into a hallway. At the end, to the right, there was a door opened halfway.

She walked to the door, pushed it open, and looked around. A large window offered diffused light through gauzy white curtains, highlighting a queen bed parallel to the window, two night tables on either side of the bed, an armoire across from the bed, and a large chair with several accent pillows to the left of the bed. A floor mirror stood in the corner diagonally across from the door.

Opposite the bed, near the door, an opening led to a short hall connecting the bedroom to the en suite bathroom. Peering into the short hall, she gasped and her heart dropped. Someone was standing in the bathroom. Paralyzed, Spencer opened her mouth to scream and then saw the person standing in the bathroom was opening her mouth. A split second later, realization dawned. She was staring at her own reflection in a framed mirror above a speckled marble counter.

Feeling stupid for being frightened by her own image, Spencer sighed and then told herself to quickly find a pen and paper and write the damn note for Maxine, so she could leave.

As she started to turn, Spencer noticed a set of accordion doors half-opened. Frowning, Spencer inched forward, her gaze drawn to the floor, toward something in the space between the doors. Her heart jerked.

It was a hand.

Lying palm up, the fingers were coated with a dark, wet substance. Blood.

A scream from the pit of her gut rose up her throat and got stuck there, leaving her gasping and coughing, trying to breathe as she stared at the severed hand on the closet floor.

Spencer rushed out into the bedroom, confused and trembling, trying to catch her breath, trying to understand what was happening. A bloody hand on the floor? What the hell? How? Why? Who had cut the hand off? Who did the hand belong to? Where was the body? Was that Maxine Porter's hand? Why would someone have cut her hand off? Who would have—

A shadowy movement in the far corner near the mirror startled her. Spencer turned toward it, looking across the room at the reflection. It wasn't her own shocked, terrified face.

With sickening horror, she recognized the face glaring back at her. Her pulse racing, she turned and—

The butt of a gun came toward her face.

28

San Pedro, Belize
Estrella Estates

Cautious, Sione walked to the stucco wall surrounding the porch of unit #309. Pushing the gate open, he tried to ignore the twinge of unease he felt as he stepped inside. His heart lurched slightly as he stared through the glass of the screen door. The front door was open. He could see straight into the condo.

Forgetting about D.J.'s warning to stay out of sight and watch from a distance, Sione opened the screen door and stepped into the condo. The pneumatic hiss of the screen door closing made him wonder if maybe his actions had been a bit too hasty. What if he was walking into some sort of ambush?

He was unarmed in unfamiliar territory. He wasn't afraid though. His anxiousness and apprehension was reserved for Ms. Edwards. He was worried about her, and right now he was more concerned with where she was and if she was okay.

He wasn't nervous about some situation he couldn't get himself out of. He could fight his way out of just about any circumstance. His father had taught him how to deal with disadvantages and handicaps during combat. All those lessons he'd struggled to forget could be lessons he might need.

Continuing into the condo, Sione looked around. It was a simple layout. The open floor plan was basically a large, rectangular space sectioned into separate kitchen, dining, and living areas.

His cell phone vibrated. Stepping into the kitchen, he pulled it from his pocket and stared at the display. *David Jones*. Sione answered.

"Where are you?" his cousin asked.

Sione gave him a quick debriefing, and then asked, "Where are you?"

"Just getting off the ferry," D.J. said. "What did you say the name of those condos was?"

"Estrella Estates," Sione said. "North side of the island."

"Who is she visiting?"

"That's what I'm trying to find out," Sione said. "I'm in the condo, but—"

"Wait, what?" D.J. asked, his voice rising. "How did you get—"

"I didn't break in," Sione said. "The door was open, and—"

A scream cut him off, coming out of nowhere, like a sucker punch.

"What was that?" D.J. demanded. "Sione, what—"

"I gotta go."

29

Screaming, Spencer staggered backward, desperate to get away. Her foot skidded and she gasped as her ankle rolled. She stumbled, trying to keep her balance but lost the battle and slipped. She hit the hardwood floor, banging her hip. Wincing, Spencer scrambled to get back to her feet, grabbing the bed table for support as she pulled herself up. Struggling to stay on her feet, she stared at the man standing in front of her, a few feet away, terrified by the green snake etched into the Asian man's pale, pitted skin.

It was Tommy Fong. The bastard who'd broken into Ben's townhouse. The asshole who Ben claimed he'd been aiming at even though he'd pointed a gun in Spencer's face. The son of a bitch who'd broken into the honeymoon casita and tried to tie her up. What the hell was Tommy Fong doing in Maxine's home?

"What do you want?" Spencer whispered. "Why are you here?"

Fong lunged at her. With a short, startled cry, Spencer reached for the lamp on the bed table, grabbed it, and swung it at Fong. He ducked, and when Spencer swung the lamp again, he grabbed the electric cord and pulled it hard. She lost her grip on the lamp, and it fell, crashing against the hardwood floor. Fong grabbed her.

"Let me go!" She tried to wrestle away from him. "Get away from me!"

He slapped her and then shoved her toward the wall. Just like her mother used to do, Spencer realized, sickened by the abrupt memory. Tiny and frail, she would crash against the thin sheetrock before dropping to the floor. Immediately, Spencer would curl into a ball, screaming in terror, desperate to protect herself, as much as she could, from the kick she knew was coming.

Fong smacked her again. Wincing in pain, she brought her knee up between his legs. Grunting, he clutched his balls, sidestepping away from her. Taking advantage, Spencer ran into the bathroom.

Glancing over her shoulder, she saw Fong stumbling to his feet. Determined, Spencer scanned the bathroom for a weapon. Spying a can of hairspray, she grabbed the can and then turned. Fong jumped toward her. Aiming the can at the crooked, yellowed teeth he bared, she sprayed, turning her face from the stream of irritant. Howling, he stumbled, fingers furiously rubbing his eyes.

He dropped the gun and Spencer dropped to the ground, reaching for the firearm. Fong swung his foot toward her hand, and the toe of his shoe connected with her wrist. Crying out in pain, Spencer grabbed her wrist as the gun slid across the floor. Fong chased it over to the armoire, then bent over, and scooped it up.

30

San Pedro, Belize
Estrella Estates

Dropping the cell phone, Sione hurried out of the kitchen and into the dining area before cutting through an opening into a hallway. Heading to the right, he rushed down the hall and through the door. Sione stopped, staring into the bedroom, anger overtaking him.

On the bed, Ms. Edwards screamed and fought, wrestling with a man who straddled her, trying to grab her hands. In the man's other hand, he held a pistol and was raising his hand as though he meant to whip her with the gun.

Disturbed and enraged, Sione crossed to the bed in two strides, grabbed the man around the back of the neck, and pulled him off the bed, away from Ms. Edwards. The man fell to the floor, screaming something in Chinese. Sione stared at the green snake on the man's face, following it from the man's forehead as it slithered down his jaw and around his chin.

It was the Asian guy who'd broken into Ms. Edwards' casita.

Sione kicked the gun from the man's grasp, then reached down, yanked the man to his feet, and slung him into the armoire across from the bed. The man struggled to get to his knees. Sione picked up the gun, then walked to the armoire, and grabbed the man.

"Who the hell are you?" Sione asked, moving his hand to the front of the man's throat, squeezing his trachea. "What are you doing here?"

Twitching and gasping, the man dug his heels into the hardwood floor, trying to pull Sione's hand away. Sione tightened his hold around the man's throat and then slammed the gun into the center of the man's face. Blood seeped from the gash above the man's left eye, igniting something within Sione, a dark instinct he didn't try to fight.

He hit the man again, crashing the pistol against the man's forehead, his jaw, and his nose, drawing blood each time steel connected with flesh. Screaming in pain, the man gasped and gurgled, his body going limp. Tossing the gun to the floor, Sione slammed his fist into the center of the man's face, over and over and over as he lost control of his rage and fed on it. The anger coursing through him was addictive and intoxicating, and he allowed it to overtake him.

"John, no!" Ms. Edwards' frantic command cut through the thick fog of rage clouding his mind. "Don't kill him!"

The trace of fear and confusion in Ms. Edwards' hoarse cry stopped him. And shamed him. As the haze of fury cleared, Sione stared at the Asian man's face, repulsed by the bloody gashes and abrasions. Recoiling from the damage he'd inflicted, Sione pushed the man away from him. Taking a deep breath, Sione faced Ms. Edwards. Standing in front of the bed, she stared at him, apprehension in her gaze.

"Ms. Edwards." He walked toward her, but she shrank away. Still, he persisted. "Are you okay?"

"What are you doing here?" she asked.

31

———

San Pedro, Belize
Estrella Estates

Waiting for John to answer, Spencer didn't know what to think. She could hardly believe he was standing in front of her. Why? How? She didn't even know how to form the questions. She just needed the answers. Nothing made sense. There was a severed, bloody hand in the closet. Maxine was nowhere to be found. Tommy Fong had attacked her. Now John was here, asking her if she was okay, and Spencer didn't know how to answer him. She didn't know what she was, except confused. And worried. And suspicious. Why was John here? Had he known about her meeting with Maxine? Had he found out somehow? But, who could have told him? And why?

Relieved, and yet wary, Spencer stared at him. The resort owner looked like an island warrior, tall and huge, with his muscles evident despite the boring beige short-sleeved polo shirt he wore, stained with smears of blood. Towering over her, John seemed savage and brutal as he fought to catch his breath, the rise and fall of his massive chest slowing steadily. But the tenderness in his hazel gaze comforted her, made her feel protected.

She would have been beaten to death, or raped, if John hadn't shown up. The resort owner had saved her life, again, and as glad as she was to see him, she couldn't stop wondering why he was here. How had he known she was at Maxine Porter's condo?

Silence stretched between them as John seemed to struggle to answer her. Was he wrestling with the truth or trying to come up with a lie? Spencer wasn't sure which would be worse, his honesty or his deception. She had a feeling neither would be—

Something lurched behind John. Panicked, Spencer's eyes darted and caught sight of Tommy Fong, wobbly on his feet, his arm outstretched, and the gun shaking in his hand.

32

Sione saw Spencer's eyes shift left and then widen with fear. Something was behind him, he realized, and turned. Pointing the gun toward them, the Asian guy smiled, revealing bloodstained teeth.

"John, he's got—"

The Asian guy squeezed the trigger.

Sione stepped in front of Spencer, trying to shield her, and glass shattered. Spencer screamed. Realizing he'd missed, the Asian man raised the pistol again. Sione turned to Spencer, grabbed her, slipped his arms around her, and dived onto the bed.

Rolling across the duvet, he heard more glass bursting as Spencer screamed against his chest, and momentum carried them over the side of the bed. Sione broke the fall as they crashed against the hardwood floor and then quickly moved on top of her, shielding her with his body as more glass popped and shattered.

More gunshots rang out. Sione lifted his head. Panes from the window above them exploded. Glass shards and chunks smashed around them, crashing against the hardwood floor. Sione winced as shards pierced his elbow and forearm.

Beneath him, Ms. Edwards squirmed and gasped, one arm slipping around his back while the other moved between their bodies, her hand trailing along his abs and up to his chest. He couldn't ignore the arousal racing through him, filling his blood with feverish heat, but he fought the lust. Rationally, he knew this was neither the time nor the place for romance, but his body couldn't help but respond to her luscious curves. Lifting his head, he realized how close they were, their bodies flush against each other and their mouths inches away.

"Get the hell off me!" She slapped him. "What the hell is your damn problem!"

"What the hell is my damn problem?" He stared at her, confused, his jaw stinging. "Did you not see that son of a bitch shooting at us?"

"Yes, I saw him shooting at us. I'm not blind!" She scowled at him. "But I didn't expect you to tackle me like some linebacker on steroids!"

"Linebacker on steroids?"

"Get off me!" She pushed at his chest.

She really was a beautiful woman, he thought, as he gazed at her, even though she was being ungrateful.

"No." He shook his head. "Not yet."

"What? Did you say no?" She stared at him. "You're not going to get off me?"

"Not until I make sure it's safe for you to get up without being shot to death."

"Do you hear any more bullets?" she asked. "He's gone."

Hesitating, Sione listened for a moment. Silence filled the room.

The smell of smoke and gunpowder floated through the air-conditioned atmosphere.

"You let him get away," Spencer said.

"I let him get away?" He stared at her. "I stopped him from killing you. I saved your life, Ms. Edwards."

"What do you want, a gold star?" she asked. "Get off me!"

Sione liked the position they were in just fine, but an erection wouldn't be appreciated, and considering the circumstances, it was inappropriate. Reluctantly, he rolled over onto his hip and then rose to his knees. Taking a deep breath, Spencer sat up.

"Are you all right?" He stood and then stepped back, giving her room. "Are you hurt?"

Fiddling with her hair, finger combing the loose strands back into a twist at the nape of her neck, she glared at him. "Am I all right? Are you serious? What the hell do you think?"

Sighing, Sione offered a hand to help her up. Refusing it, she staggered to her feet and sank down on the edge of the bed. She shook her head, then shuddered, and leaned forward, bracing her hands on her knees.

"I was just trying to get you out of the way," he said, worried, wondering if he had accidentally hurt her. "I didn't mean to be rough. I just didn't want you to get killed. But forgive me. Next time, I'll just stand there and let you get shot at."

She cut her eyes to him. "Next time, instead of trying to save the day, why don't you make sure the bad guy doesn't get away. Some damn hero you are. This is the second time you let that guy get away!"

Her admonishment pissed him off. It wasn't because of the ungrateful attitude, but because what she'd said was true. He wasn't a hero. Even when he tried, he messed it up.

"I don't understand," she said. "You beat the guy like he stole something. He was down for the count, but instead of covering him while I called the cops, which is what I was about to do—"

"You didn't look like you were about to call the cops," he said. "You looked like you were about to have a damn nervous breakdown."

"—you decide to ask me if I was okay?"

"Excuse me for giving a damn!"

"It was obvious I wasn't okay," she said. "That asshole was about to hit me in the face with a gun when you pulled him off me—"

"You're welcome," he said.

Exhaling, she said, "You think saving my life makes up for the fact that you let a murderer get away?"

"Murderer?" He frowned, his pulse jumping. "What are you talking about?"

"I'm talking about Maxine Porter," she said, her aggressive façade starting to crack, threatening to shatter as tears filled her eyes. "I think he killed her and you let him get away!"

33

––––––––––

San Pedro, Belize
Estrella Estates

Sitting on the edge of the bed, Spencer alternated from looking down at her canvas shoes to glancing, every now and then, over toward John.

Standing in the short hall between the bedroom and the bathroom, he looked down at the bloody hand on the floor. Spencer wondered what he was thinking. Wondered when he would call the damn cops. Wondered most of all if he believed the lie she'd told him about why she'd come to see Maxine.

His hazel eyes had been expressionless when she'd explained her reason for being at the condo. She couldn't tell if he was buying what she was selling, but Rae had always told her to get her story straight and then stick to it. Never deviate from your lie, her older sister had told her. Never admit to anything. Deny, deny, deny.

Spencer took a deep breath as the day's horrible events looped in her mind again from the call from Maxine to the nauseating ride on the ferry to discovering the bloody hand, which had probably been severed from Maxine Porter's dead body, which her killer had probably buried somewhere.

The severed hand had shocked and traumatized her. Tommy Fong's attack had terrorized her.

For some reason, what really stuck in Spencer's mind was John. He hadn't explained what the hell he was doing at Maxine's condo or how he'd known Spencer would be there. His evasiveness worried her. She had a feeling he had suspicions of her, but she didn't want to jump to any conclusions. She didn't think John knew about the boxes of prescription medications or the money inside them. How could he? Unless he'd opened one of the Xanax boxes. She glanced at John again.

He was crouched next to the hand, peering intently. What the hell was he looking at? Or was he looking for something? Clues? Why would he need to look for clues? She'd told him who had killed Maxine Porter and then cut her hand off. Tommy Fong. The man he'd let get away.

Spencer had responded to John's "heroic" actions with baleful histrionics, but only because she hadn't wanted him to know the truth. When he'd grabbed her and wrapped his arms around her, she'd felt like the wind had been knocked from her, but not in the awful way that left you feeling sick and gasping for air. She'd felt dizzy and breathless, as though a surge of adrenaline and dopamine had shot through her, as if she was plunging head first into something hypnotic and exciting.

Crazy, foolish thoughts, she knew. They were still swirling in her mind, making it hard to concentrate on the current situation, which was the severed hand in the closet. Not even a gruesome dismemberment and a dangerous fugitive could steal Spencer's attention from the memories.

She and John had rolled across the bed, swirling and tumbling. After a quick drop to the floor, she'd landed on top of him. Before Spencer had a second to enjoy it, he'd switched their positions and covered her body with his. It had been hard not to wrap her arms around his neck and her legs around his waist. He was heavy on top of her, but in the best possible way, and she was even more aware of how muscular he was.

Everything about him was huge and hard. She'd had irrational, irresponsible thoughts in those moments. It was crazy, but she'd wanted him to make love to her—right there on the floor in the three feet of space between the bed and the window. And she hadn't cared about Maxine's severed hand in the closet or Tommy Fong shooting at them.

Massaging the spot between her eyes, Spencer told herself to focus. Now was not the time for romance. John was going to call the police, and she needed to think of what she would tell the San Pedro cops. It wouldn't be the truth, but it would be her story, and she planned to stick to it.

34

––––––––––

San Pedro, Belize
Estrella Estates

"Ms. Edwards, this is my cousin," John said. "David Jones."

Spencer said, "hi,", but she didn't extend a hand.

John's cousin had his arms folded and didn't look as though he thought she was good enough for him to uncross them. Tall and imposing, David Jones had the same body type as the resort owner. Vaguely, Spencer wondered if having lots of muscles was some genetic trait in John's family. His cousin seemed to be an alternate version of him, one dipped in dark chocolate instead of caramel.

"He works in security," John said.

Spencer nodded, but she was completely confused. Why hadn't John called the cops? What was his security guard cousin supposed to do?

Moments ago, she'd seen John walk into the closet, disappearing from her view, and when he'd walked out, he'd been on the phone.

Spencer had assumed he was talking to the police. She tried to calm down and mentally prepare herself to tell her story to the cops as convincingly as possible with a straight face. Minutes later, there was a knock at the door, and John went to answer it.

Spencer had stood up and paced across the bedroom a few times, trying to calm her nerves. Turned out, she shouldn't have bothered. The guy who'd walked into the room wasn't a uniformed deputy.

As David looked her up and down, there was a faint smile on his face, but she couldn't tell if he appreciated her looks or not. His dark gaze had lingered a bit on her breasts, but he didn't make her feel sexy, the way John did. Instead, David looked at her as though he knew some secret she was hiding, which made her think of the box she'd delivered to Maxine Porter a few days ago. She wondered if John had found out about the money and passports.

"So, Ms. Edwards," David said. "Why don't you tell me what happened here today."

"I don't understand," she said and then glanced at John.

"What don't you understand?" David asked.

"I don't understand why I have to tell you anything," she said, her voice shrill. "John, I thought you were going to call the police."

David frowned. "Who is John?"

"I'm John," the resort owner told his cousin.

"You're John?" David gave John a strange look. "Since when?"

"It's a long story," John said, looking a bit embarrassed and uncomfortable. "Anyway, Ms. Edwards, David is a private investigator. So, I thought maybe he could help us with the situation."

"Why do we need help with the situation?" Spencer asked, suddenly wary. "We just need to explain the situation to the police."

The cousins glanced at each other, exchanging a look. Spencer was beginning to think they didn't want to call the police. She was thinking their reluctance to get the cops involved had something to do with the reason why John had shown up at Maxine's condo just in time to save her from Tommy Fong. Again, she went back to wondering if John knew about the money and passports.

"Do you know who lives in this condo?"

"A woman named Maxine Porter."

"She a friend of yours?" David asked.

"We're not friends," Spencer said. "I met her a few days ago at a boutique on Front Street. She works there as a sales assistant."

"You're not friends but you came all the way from San Ignacio to San Pedro to visit her?" David asked.

"I wasn't coming to visit her," Spencer said. "I accidentally left my driver's license in the store, and she called me and told me I could come and get it from her."

"Really?" David cocked his head, eyes narrowed. "So, you left your identification at the store, but she wanted you to come to her condo to get it? Strange."

"Well, she wasn't working today," Spencer improvised, trying to keep her tone even and casual. "And she knew I needed my identification, so she offered to let me come and pick it up from her condo, which I think was actually nice of her and not strange at all."

"Strange that she took your identification from the store," David said, glaring down at her. "Most times, when customers accidentally leave their IDs or credit cards at a store, the employees will lock those items in a safe, or some other secure place, until the customers come back for them."

Spencer shrugged, trying to think of something plausible. "Well, I don't know why she took my ID home with her. Maybe she accidentally did that. All I know is, I wanted my driver's license, so I told her I would come to her condo and get it."

"And when you got here, did she give you the driver's license?"

Spencer looked up at David. "When I got here, she wasn't here."

"Then how did you get into the condo?"

"The door was unlocked," Spencer said and then sat on the edge of the bed.

"And you just walked in?" David asked.

"I knocked first, but she didn't answer," Spencer said. "So I decided to come inside and leave her a note."

"Where is the note?"

"I didn't get a chance to write it," she said, frustrated by his questions, afraid her answers sounded like farfetched lies. "I found the bloody hand, and ..."

"So I'm assuming there's nobody who can corroborate your story?"

"It's not a story, it's the truth," Spencer said. "And I don't need anybody to corroborate it."

"Can you prove that the hand you saw on the floor was severed from its body when you arrived at the condo?" David asked.

"Wait a minute," Spencer glared at John's cousin, her heart slamming. "Do you actually think I killed Maxine and cut her hand off?"

"No, he doesn't think that," John said. "He's just—"

"I'm just trying to figure out what happened," David said. "It's entirely possible that Ms. Edwards arrived at the condo and she and Maxine Porter had an altercation of some kind and Ms. Edwards killed Ms. Porter and then—"

"Go to hell!" Spencer told him.

"The cops are going to ask you the same questions," David said. "And if you get that defensive attitude with them—"

"Excuse us," John said, then put his hand on the back of his cousin's neck, and pushed him. Only David didn't budge and John had to struggle to force him, cursing and protesting, out of the bedroom and down the hall.

Jumping up from the bed, Spencer tiptoed to the door and peeked out into the hall. John and his cousin headed back into the living area of the condo. Spencer dashed down the hall, as quietly as possible, then stopped near the opening into the living room, and listened.

"Take it easy on her," John was saying.

"Take it easy on her?" David said, his tone incredulous. "Do I have to remind you—"

"She's been through a lot."

"And everything she's been through," David said, "I'm sure she brought on herself."

Spencer rolled her eyes. She hadn't brought anything on herself. She hadn't invited death and violence into her life. On second thought, maybe John's cousin was right. Technically, her past mistakes had led her to this condo where she'd discovered a bloody hand and had nearly been killed herself. But she didn't like David's accusatory attitude.

"Will you just cut her some slack?"

"What is it with you and this woman?" David asked.

Spencer waited to hear John's answer.

"What the hell are you talking about?" John asked. "There's nothing with me and her. I just don't think she's in any shape to be interrogated."

"That's why you didn't call the cops?"

"I was actually about to call them when you showed up."

"Yeah, right," David said and then laughed softly. "But it's probably good you didn't. We don't need both of you lying to the cops."

"What would I lie to the cops about?"

"Maybe about what you're doing here," David said. "You can't tell the cops that because then she'll know—"

"Yeah, I know," John said.

She'll know … what? Spencer wondered. What was David going to say?

"What did you tell her when she asked why you were here?"

He didn't.

"I didn't tell her anything," John said. "I sort of evaded the question."

Ignored the question was more like it.

"You're not going to be able to duck and dodge forever," David said. "She's going to want to know what you were doing here."

"I'll come up with something," John said.

So, he's going to lie to me.

"So, you're going to lie to her like she lied to you," David said. "Nice way to start a relationship."

"What relationship?" John asked. "I'm not getting involved with this woman."

Spencer frowned, worried. She was supposed to get close to the resort owner, but not too close. If he didn't want to get involved with her, his reluctance might affect her ability to do the favor for Ben.

But they could get close without getting involved.

And she wasn't supposed to get involved with the resort owner. *Close, but not too close,* those had been Ben's instructions. Spencer didn't even want to get involved with John so who the hell cared if he didn't want to get involved with her?

"I hope you don't get involved with her," David said. "I get the feeling she's a ho you don't need to bother saving, Captain."

35

San Ignacio, Belize
Belizean Banyan Resort

"I think you should stay with me," John announced.

Puzzled and wary, Spencer glanced up at him as they walked along the gravel-and-stone path through the resort. "Stay with you?" Spencer was confused, suspicious. "You mean ... in your casita?"

"There's more than enough room," he said. "The owner's casita is actually the original hotel my uncle bought. It was just a small boutique place with five suites. A few years later, he began building the casitas, and he converted this place into his residence. It's got seven bedrooms, so ..."

Two hours had passed since the strange, terrible events in San Pedro. It was close to three in the afternoon, and they were now back in San Ignacio, courtesy of the spacious, luxurious Belizean Banyan water taxi, which had taken them across the turquoise waters to the ferry, where a resort shuttle was waiting to drive them back to the resort.

The cloudy skies of Ambergris Caye had been left behind. The sun was out in San Ignacio, warm and bright, and the air was fragrant with allspice, roses, and dense, rich vegetation. It was a perfectly beautiful lazy afternoon, but Spencer couldn't enjoy it. She couldn't stop thinking about what had happened in Maxine Porter's condo.

Her thoughts flickered and skipped from the bloody hand on the floor in the closet to Tommy Fong's vicious attack to John's confusing presence at the condo and then looped back to the hand on the closet floor.

There were too many questions. Hardly any answers. Where the hell was Maxine Porter? Was that her hand in the closet? Was her dead body buried somewhere?

Had Tommy Fong followed her to the condo? Did Fong's attack have something to do with the animosity between him and Ben?

Why had John shown up at the condo? He hadn't answered her question.

Spencer had overheard him talking to his cousin, and she didn't think John would be honest with her.

Why had John called his cousin instead of the police? And why did she get the feeling John and his cousin knew more about her than they were admitting?

"Thank you, but I don't think that's a good idea," Spencer said, cutting her eyes up at him. "I think I should go back to the honeymoon casita."

John shook his head. "I don't think that's a good idea."

"Why not?" Spencer asked. "I'm not afraid to be alone."

"I don't want you to be alone," he said, guiding her down a path near the forest, between clusters of oleander and hibiscus bushes which provided a tropical cocoon for the casitas hidden behind their vibrant flowers and verdant leaves. "I don't think it's safe for you to be by yourself tonight. The son of a bitch with the snake on his face got away."

"You think he might be waiting for me at the honeymoon casita?"

"I wouldn't put it past him," John said. "The guy has come after you twice. He seems determined to hurt you for some reason."

Spencer looked away, wary of the insinuation in John's tone, wondering if he suspected she knew why Tommy Fong had targeted her but wasn't admitting it.

"I just think it would be safer for you if you stayed with me tonight."

"I don't need you to rush in and save me, okay?" She said, hoping her belligerence would distract him from any further inquiries about Fong's reasons for attacking her. "I don't need you to keep me safe from harm. I don't need a hero."

"Well, you're in luck," he said. "Because I'm not exactly a hero."

"I figured you weren't," she snipped, even though she was sort of touched by and grateful for his offer to take care of her. He seemed sincere, and though she wouldn't admit it, there was something nice about him doing something for her out of the goodness of his heart.

And, of course, staying with him in his casita could help her complete *Step Two*.

"Besides, I want to have security check out the honeymoon casita," he said. "And I want to have more cameras installed around the perimeter. Most of all, I just want you to be okay. You've been through a lot today, and I know it was rough for you. I want you to be safe and trust me and let me help you."

His words shocked her. She wasn't surprised at his sentiment and sympathy. She was astounded because he'd said something she had never thought she would hear someone tell her. She'd never believed anyone would be there for her when she needed it the most.

Spencer felt close to tears, which was ridiculous; tears didn't matter.

She knew, from experience, you could cry all night, and still no one would come—not for her—no one had ever shown up to wipe the tears away. It was pointless to play the victim or complain or be upset about being neglected and abandoned by the people she'd counted on the most.

She was hesitant, nervous, and reluctant to take advantage of John's selfless hospitality; she wanted to be suspicious of his gracious offer, wanted to keep her guard up. Spencer didn't want to get too comfortable in his surroundings. She didn't want to start thinking she could rely on him to keep his word, even though she had a feeling he would.

Somehow, his trustworthiness didn't put her mind at ease.

"Okay, I'll stay," she said. "But just for one night."

36

Sione stood in the office casita, staring at his desk. It was cluttered with things he hadn't gotten around to doing. Mundane administrative things. Invoices. Proposals. Payroll. There was plenty to do, but he couldn't concentrate. The burden of what had happened in condo 309 at Estrella Estates weighed heavily on his mind. The burden of knowing the truth about the severed hand.

At least, Sione thought he knew the truth. He had a pretty good idea who had chopped it off, but he hoped he was wrong because if he wasn't, then …

Then he would have to tell the cops.

Sione sat and grabbed an invoice as the leather seat creaked beneath his weight. If he avoided finding out the truth about whoever had left the severed hand behind, then he wouldn't be forced to reveal it. Which was cowardly, he knew. Rubbing his jaw, Sione focused on the invoice, hoping to use it as another distraction.

After he and Ms. Edwards had returned to the resort two hours ago, around three o'clock in the afternoon, Sione had been distracted by the focus of taking care of her. She'd been through hell; the severed hand and the attack on her life had taken a toll. Fatigue and mental anguish had made her apprehensive and distrustful. Worried about her state of mind, Sione had insisted she return to the owner's casita so she could rest. And so he could watch her. He didn't want anything bad to happen to her again.

Sione didn't think the guy with the snake tattoo would be stupid enough to come back a third time, but, just in case, he didn't want Spencer in the honeymoon casita, where the guy would most likely look for her.

Once he'd gotten Spencer settled in one of the guest rooms, he'd struggled to find something to take his mind off the day's strange, tragic events. Without the distraction of making sure Spencer was comfortable and felt safe, he'd turned to work to take his mind away from the events in San Pedro. And now, all of sudden, for whatever reason, his cousin Peter had slipped into his head.

Sione tossed the invoice back on the desk. When D.J. had told him Peter's name was on the list of Moana's visitors, Sione hadn't known what to think. When the hell had Peter gone to see her? Why wouldn't Peter tell him about visiting Moana?

Why the hell was he sitting there speculating?

Rubbing his eyes, Sione sighed. He needed answers. He needed to talk to Peter.

37

____

San Ignacio, Belize
Belmopan

"I need to talk to you." Sione stared down at Peter Rios, who was sitting on an overturned wooden crate beneath a large allspice tree.

His fingers wrapped around a long-necked bottle of Bud Light, Peter looked up and gave Sione a baleful sneer.

"Did you hear me?" Sione said. "I said I need to talk to you."

Peter took a swig of beer and looked toward the house, which wasn't much more than a shack constructed of mostly rotting wood. Sione followed the sullen teenager's laconic gaze to an older woman sitting on the crumbling concrete porch step, braiding several strips of leather into something she probably planned to sell at a roadside flea market.

Frustrated, Sione sighed. He could think of a dozen things he could be doing right now, and a visit to his ambivalent, apathetic cousin was not one of them. But he needed distraction from thoughts about the bloody hand found in Maxine Porter's condo. And he wanted to know why the hell Peter had visited Moana in prison.

Sione stared at Peter, who appeared to be concerned only with the malted hops in his long-necked bottle. Sione suspected it was all an act, though—a defense mechanism against the frustration of unemployment and boredom.

"Why did you visit Moana in prison?"

Peter's lip curled in derision and then he took a sip of beer. "I don't know what you talking about."

"The hell you don't," Sione said. "You went to visit her. Why did you do that?"

Peter frowned. "Who told you I went to see Moana?"

"Tell me why you went to see her," Sione said.

"I don't know who told you that, but I didn't go to see her." Peter took a few more furtive sips of the Bud Light. "Somebody must have gave you the wrong information."

Sione snatched the beer bottle away from Peter, then clamped his hand around his cousin's neck, and yanked the lying punk to his feet. Protesting and cursing, Peter tried to pull Sione's hand away, but it was no use. Sione forced him around the side of the house, away from the old woman watching them, and then threw his cousin against the rotting plywood, pinning him there.

"Tell me why you went to see her," Sione demanded.

"Man, get off me." Peter struggled to push Sione's arm back. "I told you, I ain't—"

"Peter, if I wanted to, I could crush your throat." Pressing his forearm against his cousin's Adam's apple, Sione stared down at him. "But I need you to tell me why you went to visit Moana, so I'm going to spare you the pain."

Eyes bugged, Peter trembled.

"Now, I'm going to take my arm away," Sione said. "And when I do, I want you to tell me why you went to see Moana, and I don't want to hear any more lies about how you didn't go to see her, because that will really piss me off, and I will have to hurt you, do you understand?"

Sweat broke out on his cousin's forehead as he nodded slowly.

Removing his arm, Sione stepped back, disappointed that he'd allowed those violent tendencies from his past to guide his actions.

Swallowing, rubbing his throat, Peter finally said, "I went to see her."

"I know you did," Sione told him. "What I don't know is why?"

"She called me and said she wanted me to come see her," Peter said. "So, I did."

"When was this?"

"About five or six months ago."

"What happened when you went to see her?" Sione asked. "What did you talk about?"

Regaining a bit of his arrogant apathy, Peter put a bit more distance between himself and Sione and then said, "She needed my help."

"With what?"

"She wanted me to get something for her," Peter said. "An envelope."

"She wanted you to get an envelope?"

"From some house in Jamaica," Peter said. "She said she would write to me and give me all the details. The letter came about two weeks later. It had the address of this house in Montego Bay."

"She wanted you to steal something from a house in Montego Bay?"

Peter shook his head. "I didn't break in. She told me where to find the key in the letter. What she needed me to get would be in a safe in the bedroom. The combination to the safe was in the letter, too."

"So, you went to the house in Montego Bay and got the envelope for her?"

Peter nodded. "Then I called her and told her I had the envelope."

"What was in the envelope?"

Peter shrugged. "I didn't open it. It was sealed, but ..."

"But what?"

"The seal was like one of those round, red seals," Peter said, struggling to explain himself. "You know like the kind that's on a really old letter? You know how they used to seal letters like hundreds of years ago?"

"A wax seal?" Sione asked.

"Yeah, a wax seal," Peter said, nodding. "The envelope was made of real fancy paper, too."

"Okay, you call Moana and tell her you have the envelope she needs," Sione said. "Then what?"

"She told me to hide it," Peter said.

"And did you?"

His cousin gave him a defiant glare, but it didn't last and was quickly replaced by shame as he said, "Yeah."

"Where?"

"Look, I only hid it because she wanted me to," Peter said. "I probably shouldn't have, but she was always nice to me. We were friends."

Exasperated, Sione said, "Peter, where the hell did you hide the damn envelope?"

"Promise you won't kill me," Peter demanded.

"Peter," Sione warned, trying to temper the frustration and anger rising within him.

Worry in his light brown eyes, Peter said, "Moana told me to hide it in your casita."

38

Strange, blaring chimes roused Spencer.

Disoriented and sluggish, she struggled to sit up and open her eyes. It took her a moment to realize she wasn't dreaming. She was awake and in a bed, the sheets damp and twisted around her body. Staring straight ahead, left, and then right, it took her a few more minutes to reason she was in a bedroom. The furnishings didn't look familiar. She wasn't in her apartment. Filled with dread, her heart lurched. Where the hell was she?

Trying not to panic, she glanced around the room again. Dim, but not completely dark. Light spilled from a door opened just enough to spark a memory within her. It was a bathroom. She'd taken a shower, and then she'd stumbled to the bed, climbed under the covers, and crashed.

The strange chimes cut through the silence again, startling her.

What was that? Her cell phone, the answer came to her. Her cell phone was ringing. Reluctantly, she slid out of bed. Where was her purse?

Spotting a lamp on the bedside table, she groped beneath the shade and turned it on. Hazy, golden light flooded the room, clearing away the temporary amnesia. She knew exactly where she was. John's casita.

After the horror show at Maxine Porter's condo, where she was nearly killed, John had insisted she come back to his casita and stay with him. He was worried Tommy Fong might come back to attack her again and the honeymoon casita would be the first place Fong would look.

Spencer had protested but not as vigorously as she could have. She'd told John she was okay, but the bloody severed hand had terrified her. Despite her brave posturing, Spencer really hadn't wanted to be alone in the honeymoon casita.

Spotting the blue Birkin on a chair in the corner, Spencer hurried to it. She opened the purse, grabbed the cell phone, and then frowned. It wasn't ringing, but she still heard the strange chimes. A second later, the source of the sound came to her. The burner phone. She had a text.

Reluctantly, she took the burner phone from the Birkin and sat on the edge of the bed. Checking the time on the phone, she was shocked she'd slept for so long—more than six hours. Stress and fear had wiped her out, mentally and physically. She supposed lapsing into a near comatose state was her body's way of responding to the terror of discovering a severed body part and being slapped around and shot at. Deciding to get it over with, since she knew who the text was from, she accessed it.

call me right now

Her heart slammed. Trembling, Spencer eased down on the edge of the bed and called Ben. When he answered on the second ring, disappointment seeped into her, spreading like poison. Spencer almost hung up the phone. Instead, she said, "Ben, I need to tell you something that happened today. Maxine Porter called me this morning, saying she wanted to see me, and when I went to her condo—"

"Sweet girl, I don't have a lot of time," Ben cut her off, his tone curt, tense. "So, listen very carefully—"

"Wait a minute," she tried to stop him. "I need to tell you—"

"Right now, we need to talk about *Step Three*."

"*Step Three?*" she echoed in disbelief. "Ben, listen to me! I think something bad happened to—"

"Are you in Sione Tuiali'i's casita right now?"

"What?"

"Are you in his casita right now?" Ben repeated.

"How do you know that?" she asked, terrified and perplexed.

"Well, I didn't find out because you told me," he said, a menacing edge to his tone. "Which was what you were supposed to do."

"I'm sorry, okay," she said. "I'm sorry, but I'm not at his casita because he invited me to dinner, I'm here because—"

"I need you to look for something," Ben said.

"You need me to ... *what?*"

"An envelope made of lambskin. Sealed with a wax stamp that has a dragon symbol."

"Wait a minute," she said, confused and flustered. "You want me to look for an envelope? Are you serious? Is that really *Step Three?*"

Ben's short exhale told her that she was trying his patience.

"Do you know how damn big this casita is?" she asked, unable to believe he actually wanted her to search for an envelope sealed with wax. "Where do I even begin to look for this envelope?"

"It's hidden somewhere in that casita," Ben said. "I need you to find it."

"Why?" she asked. "What's in that envelope that you need so bad?"

"Hold on, hold on," he interrupted, and she heard other voices in the background, speaking a language she couldn't make out at first. A few minutes later, she heard Ben's reply, a frustrated command, and she realized he was speaking Jamaican patois.

"Sweet girl, listen," he said, his voice loud and frustrated as he spoke above the din of competing voices. "Let me know—"

"Ben, where are you?"

"—when you get *Step Three* done," he said. "I have to go."

"Wait, don't hang up," she said. "I need to tell you about—"

A string of rapid-fire patois burst forth, wild and angry, making her pulse jump, making her wonder where Ben was, what was going on, and if he was okay.

"Ben …" she said, her heart thudding as she waited for his reply. "Ben … are you still there?"

She heard more boisterous patois, and then the line went dead.

Puzzled, Spencer wondered if Ben was all right.

If something happened to Ben, how would she get her passport back? She'd have to deal with the hassle of getting new identification. And who would pay for the honeymoon casita? Who would pay for her plane ticket back to Houston?

She hadn't understood all the loud, belligerent patois, but it scared her. Was Ben caught up in some dangerous situation he might not get out of alive? Despite herself, she was concerned about him. Not that he deserved her nervous hand wringing or her prayers. Ben Chang could take care of himself. Sighing, Spencer clutched the burner phone, trying to make sense of *Step Three*.

A lambskin envelope with a wax seal featuring some kind of

dragon motif? What the hell? What was in the envelope? And how did Ben know it was in John's casita? How did he know—

"Ms. Edwards …"

Gasping, Spencer shuddered and turned. The resort owner stood in the doorway, staring at her.

"Oh my God!" Spencer pressed a hand against her stomach, afraid it might leap up out of her throat. "Are you trying to scare me to death?"

Wearing nothing but one of those sarongs tied around his waist, John was shirtless, showing off all his muscles, giving her thoughts she didn't have time to deal with right now, thoughts she couldn't reconcile. Lust intruded on the irritation and frustration of *Step Three*.

I need you to look for something … it's hidden somewhere in that casita.

"I'm sorry." John walked toward her. "I didn't mean to scare you. I thought—"

"What do you want?"

"I came to check on you," he said. "I heard you talking. Were you on the phone?"

"What?" she asked and then remembered the burner phone in her hand. Clutching it tighter, she said, "I was trying to call my sister, but I had to leave a message."

"Are you okay?"

"Not really." She looked at the floor. "But I will be."

"I was going to make a little dinner," he said. "Are you hungry?"

Spencer looked up, shocked to find he'd stepped closer to her— too close, into her personal space. She should step back, she knew. She wasn't supposed to get too close. "No, I'm all right," she said. "I just want to try to rest again."

"Okay, well," he said, "I'll be in the kitchen if you need anything."

When he left, Spencer hurried to the door and locked it. Staring at the door, she struggled to shift her thoughts away from the resort owner and how good it felt being closer to him than she should have been. She had to forget about John right now. She had to focus on the favor she needed to do for Ben. She hadn't realized she'd completed *Step Two*. Now, Ben expected her to accomplish *Step Three*?

I need you to look for something.

She had to find a damn envelope, which could be anywhere—even in the very room she was standing in.

39

Sitting on the edge of the bed, Spencer checked the time on the burner phone again. Nearly a quarter after midnight. Standing, she paced the length of the room, trying to come up with a game plan for her search.

Moments ago, she'd slipped out of the guest room and crept around the casita, trying to come up with a mental blueprint. Casing the joint, she supposed it was called. The place was massive, but she discovered the maze of rooms was manageable.

She could probably start with the bedrooms tonight. She'd already searched the bedroom she was staying in and had come up with nothing, despite searching every corner and crevice. Spencer rubbed her left temple. There were two more bedrooms on this wing. Around the corner to her right was another wing where the remaining three bedrooms were.

Tomorrow, Spencer planned to see if she might be able to stick around while John went to his office at the administration building. If so, she could check the rest of the house—living room, den, dining room, John's office, and the master suite, which seemed to be in its own separate wing.

Opening the door to her guest suite, Spencer peeked out into the long, wide hallway, looking left and then right. It was dark, but wall sconces provided just enough light to keep her from tripping over herself. Hurrying across the hall, she went into the second bedroom and quickly searched it, checking the bedside tables, the dresser, and the chest. She opened every drawer and each one was empty. Finally, she checked the closet, but there was nothing but a few empty hangers.

Fighting panic, Spencer went to the third bedroom and followed the same routine. She went through the two nightstands, the dresser, and the bureau drawers. There was a bookshelf in the room, and she searched it, pulling down all the books and flipping through the pages, praying the envelope had been slipped between a copy of *Love in the Time of Cholera* or *The Strange Case of Dr. Jekyll and Mr. Hyde* or the leather-bound *King James Bible*. The bookshelf was a bust.

Spencer went into the closet. More empty hangers and a seven-drawer chest at the back of the closet. She hurried to the bureau. The damn thing was almost as tall as she was. Or, almost as short, she supposed, opening the top drawer. Standing on her toes, she glanced inside. Empty. She closed it and pulled out the next drawer. Nothing. Exhaling in frustration, she pulled out the third drawer, figuring there would be nothing—

She gasped, her heart slamming. There were a dozen or so dolls inside the drawer. Barbie dolls. Some were clothed. Others were nude. A few were half-dressed. And they were all nationalities. White. Asian. Hispanic. Black.

Not so fast, Black Barbie.

The freckle-faced tomboy's warning faded and was replaced by another memory.

Did you hear me? I told you to cut the light off and go to bed! Why don't you ever do what I tell you to do! Give me that damn doll!

Trembling, Spencer inched her hand toward the dolls.

40

Sione walked out of his bedroom and into the hallway.

It was well after midnight, and he was tired as hell, but he couldn't sleep. He couldn't relax and couldn't force the events of the day out of his head. The bloody hand in San Pedro battled with Peter's story about an envelope Moana had told him to hide in his casita. But Ms. Edwards caused the most apprehension.

What would have happened if he hadn't gotten there in time to stop the Asian guy from hurting her? That "what if" plagued him, so much that it had driven him out of bed. The intrusive worries about Ms. Edwards forced him to check on her. She was probably okay, but Sione had to make sure. He needed to see for himself that she was resting peacefully in the guestroom.

Heading across the casita, wall sconces gave off dim light, preventing him from stumbling into anything as he made his way to the guestroom where Ms. Edwards was sleeping. At her door, he knocked softly and then opened it. "Ms. Edwards?" There was no answer. Ms. Edwards wasn't in the room. The bed was empty and the bathroom light was off. Sione glanced at the bed again. The bed linens were in disarray, as though she'd gotten out of bed and pushed the covers back. Where was she?

Back in the hallway, Sione saw faint light coming from inside the bedroom at the end of the hall. Confused, he headed to the bedroom and slipped through the half-opened door. Drawn by the glow of light coming from the closet, he walked toward it.

41

"Ms. Edwards …"

Jumping slightly, Spencer turned and looked up, heart pounding.

John stood in the entrance to the closet, staring at her. "What are you doing in here?"

Staring at him, Spencer clutched the doll. "Nothing," she stammered, her voice barely above a whisper. "I mean, I was—"

"What are you doing with that doll?" John walked toward her, frowning a bit.

"I was, um." She stared at the doll, trying to catch her breath, fighting to suppress the painful memories threatening to overtake her. "I was looking for something more comfortable to sleep in than this tank top and these shorts, and I opened this drawer and saw all those dolls."

"Those are for the girls when they come over," he said. "I keep all these things in that bureau drawer."

Nodding, Spencer turned, then put the doll back in the drawer, and closed it.

"I'm sorry," John said. "I should have had someone get your things from the honeymoon casita."

"That's okay," she said, not yet ready to face him, still fighting the effects of that horrible memory which shouldn't have had the power to bring her to her knees. And yet, she was finding it very difficult to hold back her tears.

"Ms. Edwards," John said. "Are you okay?"

Unable to speak, Spencer nodded again and squeezed her eyes shut, trying to prevent the tears from falling. Moments later, she felt his hands on her shoulders. Turning her away from the chest, he slipped his finger slipped beneath her chin and lifted her head.

"Why are you crying?"

"I'm not crying," she insisted as she opened her eyes and a tear fell down her face.

"What's the matter?" he asked, gently running a thumb across her cheek. "Are you upset because—"

"Nothing, it's just ..." She sighed and moved away from him, afraid of what would happen if she got too close. "That damn doll."

"The doll made you cry?"

Hesitating, she looked up at him as he gazed down at her, and she felt something strange and poignant, like maybe John might be interested in her. Which was ridiculous, she knew. John wasn't interested in her. Not really.

Well, he might be interested in having sex with her, but he probably wasn't interested in anything beyond that. He wasn't interested in really getting to know her or understanding her. He wasn't interested in what her hopes and dreams were. If he ever found out why she was really in Belize, all he'd be interested in was calling the cops on her.

"Of course not," she snapped, swiping the tears from her face, worried she'd accidentally said too much. "It's just something about those dolls reminded me of that hand I found in Maxine Porter's closet."

"I'm sorry you had to go through all that," he said. "I know it wasn't easy."

"I don't want to talk about it," she said and faced him. "I just want to know if you have something I can sleep in?"

Nodding, he said, "I have some T-shirts in my room."

42

<hr>

"Well, thanks for this," Spencer said, walking out of John's bathroom, where she'd just changed into one of his T-shirts, which drowned her, as she'd suspected it would. "And goodnight."

Quickly, Spencer headed toward the double doors, wondering if she should risk checking the other three bedrooms, or—

"Ms. Edwards, wait a minute."

Spencer stopped and then looked over her shoulder. John was walking to her.

"What is it?" she asked, facing him.

"I think you should stay in here," he said.

"In your bedroom?"

"I don't like it that you're on the opposite side of the casita."

"Um, Mr. Tuiali'i—

"John," he said, smiling slightly as he corrected her.

Pleasantly surprised at his use of her adopted name for him, Spencer said, "John, I don't want you to get the wrong idea. I know that we, um … we kissed that one time, but we both had way too much to drink, and I really am not interested in—"

"Neither am I," he interrupted. "But I am interested in getting some sleep, and I don't think I'm going to be able to do that unless I can be sure that you're safe and nothing bad will happen to you."

Spencer hesitated, not sure what to say.

"Look, I know it may seem like I'm just trying to get you into bed," he said.

"But you are trying to get me into bed," she teased.

"So we can both get some rest," he said. "And I'll sleep in the chair if that will make you feel more comfortable."

"You don't have to do that," she said, sneaking a peek at the California king. "Anyway, that bed is huge. I think it's big enough for the both of us."

Moments later, John pulled the duvet back, and Spencer stared at the crisp sheets, hesitating. Getting in bed with the resort owner was risky, like slipping into something both enticing and dangerous. Once she got into bed with John, Spencer had a feeling she would be enveloping herself into something she might not be able to get out of, something she wouldn't be able to resist. Getting in bed with him might be getting too close. She was only supposed to get just close enough.

Maybe she was making too much of the situation. They were going to be sleeping together but not sleeping together. She wasn't going to be making love with John. She would only be making it possible for him to get some rest. He was worried about her. He was afraid Tommy Fong might attack her again, and he might be too far to get to her in time to stop the assault.

Spencer climbed into the bed. As John walked around to the other side of the bed, Spencer pulled the covers up to her neck and tried to get settled beneath the duvet. The bed was warm, even though the sheets were cool and crisp and obviously expensive, probably a million-thread count or something equally ridiculous.

As she turned over onto her side and laid her cheek against the pillow, an intoxicating scent swirled around her, seeping into her. The smell seemed to manifest into something tangible, caressing her as she struggled to ignore the feeling.

There was a small click and darkness cloaked the room. John had turned off the lamp on the night table. The mattress moved and something very large seemed to have gotten into the bed with her. She tried to close her eyes and relax, but it was impossible to ignore John's presence. It was overwhelming and magnetic, as though something was pulling her toward him.

She turned over onto her back and stared at the ceiling. Light from the outdoor sconces on the terrace filtered into the room through the French doors, but she still needed a moment for her eyes to adjust to the darkness. Without turning her head, Spencer cut her gaze to the right, sneaking a glance at him. Horizontal, John seemed even more massive. It was like being in bed with a huge, hunky giant.

She felt very small and insignificant and, strangely, as though she needed protection, some sort of shelter, the kind she could only find in his arms, which was ridiculous, and yet … after a moment's hesitation, she inched over onto her right side. Her heart jumped into her throat. John was lying on his side, facing her, but his eyes were closed.

She felt out of control, as though she might do something wild and reckless, like she might get too close to him. She couldn't help herself. She was seeking the comfort of an embrace he hadn't offered. Something was inviting her to come closer to him, and she moved beneath the covers, slowly and stealthily, praying she wouldn't disturb his sleep. She stopped and waited, her heart pounding. A moment later, she scooted forward again, just an inch or so, moving even closer to him and farther away from where she'd been at the edge of the bed. Spencer slid closer to him. John's eyes flickered, the lids lifting. She squeezed her eyes shut and went still.

43

Sione didn't remember Ms. Edwards being so close to him. Hadn't she been way on the other side of the bed? As far away from him as she could possibly be? When she'd first slipped between the covers, she'd huddled near the edge, and he worried she might roll over and fall to the floor in the middle of the night.

Sione knew she wasn't too comfortable with sleeping in his bed. Maybe he shouldn't have imposed his fears and worries on her, forcing her into a situation she wasn't used to, an environment she wasn't sure she could trust. He didn't regret asking her to stay with him. Already, Sione felt his headache subsiding and the knots in his neck loosening, the tension fading. He was relaxed; sleep would soon claim him.

He wasn't ready to close his eyes. He wasn't ready to stop staring at Ms. Edwards, even though he couldn't really see her features. The light from the terrace was behind her, and he couldn't tell if she was awake. From the even rhythm of her breathing, he figured she was sleeping. Despite himself, Sione reached his arm toward her and laid his palm on her shoulder. She didn't stir beneath the weight of his hand.

Her lack of movement made him feel bold and gave him the courage to slip an arm around her. Driven by instinct and desire, he pulled her closer to him, enticed by the silkiness of her skin and her breasts beneath his T-shirt, large and round and soft with the nipples like pearls, pressed against his abs.

For some crazy reason, Sione felt as though she belonged next to him, as though holding her was the most natural thing in the world. He didn't understand his feelings; they were hard to process, unable to be qualified or quantified. He didn't understand the need to have her next to him. Cursing softly, he sighed, pissed by his thoughts. Maybe he was suffering strange effects from the trauma of the day. Maybe—

"John."

Sione froze, waiting for Ms. Edwards to realize he had his arms around her and then demand to know why the hell he was holding her. He suspected she would insist he take his damn hands off her and maybe she would slap him. A moment later, she moved her head to rest against his chest.

"Yeah," he said, holding himself still as she settled next to him.

"I didn't tell you the truth about the doll."

"What?"

"You remember when you found me in the closet and I was crying?"

"Yeah."

"It was because of those dolls," she said. "They didn't really remind me of that bloody hand. The dolls made me think of something sad that happened to me a long time ago, when I was seven."

He felt her leg on top of his thigh, sliding up and down against his skin, and he tried not to think about how much he wanted to make love to her.

"My grandmother gave me a doll for Christmas," she said. "It was a Barbie doll, a black one. My grandmother said I was as pretty as that doll."

Prettier than a doll, he thought, staying quiet and wondering how her story would end, though he suspected she was coming to a moment of sadness and heartbreak.

"I sort of fell in love with that doll," she said. "I played with that doll every day until … one day, my mother got upset with me because she'd told me to go to bed and I was still in my room with the light on, playing with my doll. She came into my room and screamed at me … and then she grabbed my doll and … she pulled the arms off, and then she pulled the legs off, and she pulled the head off … and then she threw it at me …"

Sione wasn't sure how to respond or what to say. He had thought she would tell him she'd lost the doll. He never would have imagined her mother had destroyed the doll in an act of irrational rage. What the hell kind of mother would do something like that? Sione had no business judging the woman, even though he hated what she'd done to her daughter. He knew about rage; he knew how anger could get the best of you and make you do things you never thought you would do, committing the most heinous acts, leaving you confused and ashamed.

"When I saw those dolls in the drawer, that memory just …"

He waited, holding her closer.

"Guess it doesn't matter," she said. "I don't even know why I told you that."

Sione wasn't sure about the reason for her confession, but he suspected she was suffering the effects of the trauma she'd experienced in the condo on Ambergris Caye. If not for the trauma, Ms. Edwards probably wouldn't have been so open and honest with him about something which was obviously so painful for her.

Sione wanted to be supportive and caring. He wanted her to know he could be trusted with her painful memories. He needed her to realize he was available if she needed someone to listen, to hold her, or even wipe away her tears. For some reason, he felt obligated to share one of his own painful childhood memories, but he didn't have any. As a child, he'd been blessed with parents who'd been both loving and attentive.

Only after his thirteenth birthday did things change. Not with his mother, though. Carmen Camareno had always, and still to this day, loved him more than life itself. His father's affection had become manic and confusing.

Richard's love began to feel obsessive, more feral than instinctual. Motivated by his hopes and schemes of turning Sione into a version of himself, Richard became consumed with teaching him lessons in cruelty and terror. Lessons Sione had never wanted to learn, though he'd paid close attention to his father's violent tutelage and had lived up to those destructive expectations.

Sione took a deep breath, trying to forget his own painful memories. Memories he could never share. As he glanced down at Ms. Edwards, he knew he wouldn't have to. She was asleep.

44

———————

San Ignacio, Belize

Belizean Banyan Resort - Owner's Casita

Sione cracked five eggs into a glass bowl, then grabbed a whisk, and started to whip the yolks and whites into a frenzy. As they expanded into fluffy curdles, he thought of putting Tabasco in the mix and then quickly decided against it.

The spicy red sauce brought the damn dismembered hand back into his head. He'd seen it before. Not the hand in Maxine Porter's condo, but a hand separated from its wrist. He knew what it might mean; he knew why the hand might have been left behind. But he might have been wrong. The severed hand might have been a message or maybe a warning. But a warning for who? Ms. Edwards? He didn't think so, but he couldn't rule out that possibility.

As for who had severed the hand, he had suspicions. Actually, he had more than suspicions. He had actually seen someone chop a hand off. More than once. And the first time he'd seen it done, he'd been horrified, though he'd pretended that it hadn't bothered him.

As he forced himself not to tremble, he pretended to understand why the hand had to be severed. The severed hand was a signature, he'd been told. Just as Picasso signed his paintings, the hand chopped from the wrist of the dead body gave credit to a specific killer. A killer Sione knew too damn well. A killer who might have murdered Maxine Porter and cut her hand off.

Nevertheless, suspicions weren't proof. He didn't want to make accusations which might potentially unleash the hell he'd managed to contain back into his life. Before he went to the cops, Sione had to know, without a doubt, who had severed that hand from its body. The only way to know for sure was to ask—

No, he couldn't do that. He didn't even want to *think* of doing that.

He forced his thoughts toward a different direction, to Moana and Peter and the envelope. Sione was still shocked and confused. He wouldn't have even believed Peter's story if he hadn't found the damn envelope exactly where Peter had confessed to hiding it.

Last night, as he'd drifted to sleep, Sione had tried to figure out why the hell Moana would tell Peter to retrieve an envelope from a house in Jamaica and then instruct him to hide it in his casita. This morning, he wondered if the hidden envelope had anything to do with Moana's claim that Richard had wanted her to steal something. Was that something the envelope from the house in Jamaica?

Moana had told him she'd refused his father's request, but she could have lied. She could have turned his father down and then turned right around and convinced Peter to get that envelope for her. Knowing that Richard wanted the envelope, Moana might have decided to use it as leverage, some kind of bargaining chip to force Richard to help her get out of prison.

A dangerous move. Moana knew better than to try to play games with Richard Tuiali'i. Maybe she'd been desperate. Because of him, Sione realized. Because he'd broken his promises to her.

He stared at the eggs and cursed, realizing they were a bit overdone. Moving the cast iron skillet from the burner grate, he turned the stove off and turned to the glass doors on the opposite side of the kitchen, looking toward the terrace.

Sunlight flooded the room, but it was no longer welcoming. It was a harsh, glaring spotlight on all his failures and mistakes, highlighting the truth he tried to hide from himself, the truth he wished were a lie.

He really hadn't wanted to help his ex-fiancée. He just wanted to prove to himself he could be the better person. He could turn the other cheek. He hadn't been able to pull it off because she didn't deserve the promises he'd made to her. And he never should have made them. Maybe he didn't know how to forgive and forget. Maybe he didn't know how to move forward without malice or spite.

He'd wanted to be compassionate and sympathetic toward her. He'd tried to follow the example his uncle had set for him, but he hadn't been able to do it. Now, there was nothing he could do for her. *She was dead.* Sighing, he rubbed his eyes.

"Good morning …"

Startled, Sione took his hand from his face and let it drop to his side. Ms. Edwards stood on the opposite side of the large slab of marble, a hint of amusement in her eyes as she stared at him.

"Good morning." He turned to the stove, grabbed the handle of a cast iron skillet, and then faced the island again. "I made eggs." After putting the skillet on a bamboo trivet, he winced as his knuckles throbbed.

"You okay?"

"Yeah …" Sione made a fist, grimacing from the slight sting of abrasions not completely healed. "My hand is still a little sore. No big deal."

Ms. Edwards walked around the island, stopped in front of him, and took his hand, staring at it.

"It's really not that bad," he said, uncomfortable with her attention to the abrasions and his swollen knuckles.

"This looks bad. Where's the first aid kit?"

Worried the bruises might remind her of how violent he'd been, he said, "Don't need—"

"John, you don't want these cuts to get infected."

He sighed. "In the cabinet under the sink."

"Okay, you go sit down."

"Ms. Edwards, you don't have to—"

"Just go sit at the table, please," she ordered, smiling a little.

Reluctantly, Sione did as he was told. He didn't like being fussed over, but watching her gave him a feeling of domesticity. There was something about the way she looked very serious, as she walked to the table, holding the first aid kit. It made him feel as though he was being looked after by a wife, which was stupid. He liked the feeling, but he didn't want to or even think he should.

Sione tried to remember he didn't really know anything about her, except what she'd presented to him, which may or may not have been true. He tried to look at Ms. Edwards from D.J.'s jaded, suspicious point of view. He couldn't.

She took a seat on his lap, which was nice, then put the kit on the table, opened it, and took out one of the bottles and a few cotton balls. Looking apologetic, but determined, she examined his cuts and bruises, and he wondered what it might be like if they were together. As crazy as that was. After soaking the cotton ball, she gave him the prettiest smile and then pressed a cotton ball on the gash across his knuckles. A fiery sting spread into the wound on his hand, damn near knocking him out.

"Motherfu—"

"Oh my God! I'm so sorry!"

Snatching his hand away, Sione bit his lip so he wouldn't scream.

"I'm sorry!" Ms. Edwards jumped off his lap and grabbed the bottle she'd poured liquid from onto the cotton ball. "Oh, no!"

"What?" Sione closed his eyes, trying to ignore the fierce burn, wondering if it would ever go away.

"I accidentally used alcohol instead of peroxide! I'm so sorry. Does it hurt bad?"

"Worse."

"God, I'm so stupid."

"You're not stupid," he said, opening one eye to glance at her. "It was an accident."

"I should have been paying attention," she grumbled. "It's bad enough that your hand is all cut and bruised because of me, and what do I do? I make it worse!"

He stared at her, astonished by the contrition in her gaze, the self-recrimination in her slumped shoulders. Not the badass, aggressive apathy he'd expected. The only reason he hadn't screamed was because he figured she would chide him, tell him to suck it up and deal with it. Her remorse made him feel bad for her.

"Come here …"

She hesitated, then stepped to him, and settled on his lap again.

He slipped an arm around her waist. "You didn't make things worse."

"Yes, I did."

"Okay, you did," he admitted and then smiled. "But not on purpose."

She didn't look convinced.

"Why did you say my hand was bruised because of you?"

"You only hurt your hand because ..." She looked down before lifting her gaze to him again. "You were fighting because of me."

"I was fighting for you."

She frowned. "Because of me."

He shrugged, not surprised she was uncomfortable with his wording. Probably thought it sounded too "heroic."

"Yesterday was the second time I fought." He stopped, noticing the wariness in her eyes, and then said, "because of you. It's kind of becoming a habit, I guess."

"A habit you should break."

"Why?"

"I don't need anyone to fight my battles," she said. "And didn't your cousin tell you not to bother trying to save a slut like me?"

"You heard us talking?" he asked, wondering exactly how much she'd heard them say.

"He said you shouldn't try to play the hero for me."

"He shouldn't have said that," Sione said. "And I don't feel the same way he does. As far as fighting because of you, I don't mind."

"You should mind," she said, dropping her gaze toward the table. "You don't even know me. Maybe I'm not worth all the scars and bruises on your hand."

"Well, maybe I would like to find out if you're worth—"

"What were you doing there?" She cut him off, scowling.

"What?" he asked, disappointed by her sudden change of subject, which he suspected was her attempt to put a barrier between his interest and her reluctance.

"Why were you at Maxine Porter's condo?" she asked. "You never told me."

"I was there to meet with the owner of the complex," he said. "As

I was leaving, I thought I saw you, so I decided to find out if it was really you."

"And you just followed me inside?"

"When I finally figured out which unit you'd gone into," he said, "I heard the scream."

"And you just rushed right in to save the day?"

"I rushed in to save your day," he said, teasing.

She rolled her eyes, but then she smiled, and it was like an invitation. Eager to accept, he leaned forward, anxious to feel her mouth on his, and—

"Good morning, cousin!"

Sione groaned, annoyed by D.J.'s deep, booming voice. Spencer squeaked, jumped up, and dashed around to the other side of the table.

"Ms. Edwards." D.J. gave her a curt nod and a stare that was suspicious, at best. "How are you this morning?"

"As well as can be expected, I suppose," she said, inching around the table in the direction of the wide opening leading out to the hallway. "Considering everything that happened yesterday."

"Speaking of what happened yesterday," D.J. said. "I wanted to ask you—"

"Can it wait?" she asked, walking backward, away from them. "I was just about to go and take a shower."

D.J. turned toward her as she continued her retreat. "Actually—"

With a smile and a wave, Ms. Edwards turned and dashed out of the kitchen.

Looking at Sione, D.J. asked, "Was it something I said?"

45

———

San Ignacio, Belize
Belizean Banyan Resort - Owner's Casita

Remembering her mental blueprint of the casita, Spencer walked quickly but quietly down a long, wide hallway, turning several corners and navigating more dimly lit hallways.

When John's cousin had walked into the kitchen, looking as though he could think of nothing better to do than interrogate her about the severed hand in Maxine Porter's condo, Spencer had decided she couldn't stand the heat. She had to get out of the kitchen before John's tall, imposing cousin intimidated her into confessing to something she would never do in a million years.

On her way to the shower, she'd decided to take a detour to John's casita office to search for the envelope, which probably should have been the first place to look. Where else but an office would an envelope be kept? Closing the doors behind her, Spencer crossed to the large desk in the center of the room and sat down in the huge leather chair. Spencer stared at the papers and files strewn across the surface and hesitated even though she couldn't waste time.

John's conversation with his suspicious security expert cousin would afford her the opportunity to search his office without the fear of being caught looking for the envelope. But they weren't going to talk all day. Eventually, John's cousin would leave, and then John would probably come back to his office, judging from all the paperwork he seemed to have left behind.

Why the hell was she stalling? Why the hell wasn't she searching like a crazy woman? Finding that damn envelope would mean she'd completed *Step Three*. Why wasn't she tearing the office upside down? *Step Three* could be the final step. Then this crazy nightmare could be over, and she could leave Belize, and … and never see John again.

Her stomach clenched at the thought, although she didn't know why. What did she care if she never saw the tall, handsome, muscular resort owner again? It wasn't as if she'd flown to Belize to be with him, so why should the idea of never seeing him again unsettle her?

She should be anxious to get *Step Three* done so she could get back to Houston, back to her normal life. She should have been ecstatic about being able to leave the country with her debt to Ben paid, free from his threats.

She couldn't seem to stop thinking about John. She couldn't stop thinking about the way he'd kissed her after they'd come back from that first trip to San Pedro, how perfect his lips had felt against hers, how much she'd wanted to drag him into the bedroom and let him do all sorts of nasty things to her, and—

Pushing the thoughts away, Spencer pulled the desk drawer out, delving a hand in the sea of paper clips and business cards, pushing aside a letter opener, a thumb drive, a pair of scissors, and a small calculator, but no lambskin envelope with a dragon motif wax seal.

Frustrated, Spencer yanked the drawer out farther, spotting a staple remover, "Sign Here" tabs, an eraser, rubber bands, neon highlighters, and the top corner of a blue file folder. Peeking at the file, she read the label: EDWARDS, SPENCER. Confused, she grabbed the file and opened it.

A small avalanche of papers fell out, floating to the floor. Placing the file back on the desk, Spencer crouched down and picked up the papers. She flipped them over. Her confusion gave way to uneasiness and shock. It was a photo of her. Standing with her arms crossed, she stood just outside the ragged circle of about fifteen people surrounding a tour guide. A photo of her on the tour she'd taken to the Mayan ruins.

Heart slamming, Spencer sank slowly into the leather chair, shuffling through the photos. She recognized the images of herself, even though she didn't know they had been taken. She hadn't realized she'd been the subject of someone's camera lens. No, not someone. John.

Spencer examined the photos, a pictography of her excursion to Xunantunich. There were pictures of her walking with the tour group, looking bored and sullen; one where she was listening to the tour guide; another showed her taking a photo of that old Austrian couple; and several were of her climbing the ruins.

Taking a deep breath, Spencer shoved the photos into the blue file, then put it back into the drawer, and closed it. Trying to contain the fear racing through her was damn near impossible, but she had to. She had to think. She had to figure out what the hell was going on. Why did John have these pictures of her? What was he going to do with them?

Taking a deep breath, Spencer forced herself to focus. The situation was as crazy as it was confusing, and she didn't really know what to think or how to feel. She didn't know whether to be panicked or angry; she didn't know if she should feel violent or violated.

There was one thing she did know. John couldn't have taken the photos of her if he hadn't followed her. So, the question was, why the hell had he tailed her to Xunantunich? There was really only one answer.

46

"Good thing I came when I did," D.J. said. "If I had shown up ten, maybe fifteen, minutes later, I might have seen the two of you screwing on the table."

"We weren't about to screw on the table," Sione said.

"I know what I saw," D.J. said. "Maybe you weren't about to screw her, but you were definitely going to kiss her."

"So what if I was? What the hell do you care?"

"Well, I don't care to have my cousin involved with some lying, scheming bitch who could have murdered a woman and cut off her—"

"Ms. Edwards didn't kill anybody," Sione said. "She wouldn't do something like that."

"And how would you know? You don't know jack crap about this woman, and I'm beginning to think you don't want to know the truth about her. You just want to bend her over the table and—"

"You want some eggs?" Sione asked, sick of his cousin's irritating innuendos about Ms. Edwards' guilt when he still didn't have any concrete proof of her involvement in anything criminal.

Sione could admit that, yes, Ms. Edwards could potentially be involved in something shady. She'd told a few lies, mostly about the contents of the banker's box, which brought him to the money. Almost a million dollars and three passports had been delivered to her, hidden in boxes of anti-anxiety pills. The passports were probably fake, but there was no evidence the money was stolen or to be used in some other criminal dealings.

There seemed to be evidence of Ms. Edwards switching beach bags with two other tourists—a blonde woman with freckles and a dark-haired, olive-skinned woman who might have been Hispanic— both of whom looked exactly like the women in the thumbnail photos on the passports. Still, there was no proof that money and passports had been in those beach bags, which was why Sione still wasn't convinced that Ms. Edwards was a criminal.

"Did you talk to Ms. Edwards?" D.J. asked, taking a seat at the island.

"Not yet," Sione said.

"What do you mean, not yet?" D.J. gave Sione a skeptical look. "You told me you would find out why she really went to Maxine Porter's condo. We both know the story about the driver's license she left at the boutique is bull."

"I'll talk to her tomorrow," Sione said.

D.J.'s glare turned dubious. "Why can't you talk to her today?"

"She's been through a lot," Sione said. "She found a severed hand, and she was attacked and almost killed."

"That was yesterday."

"She's still upset," Sione said. "It was very traumatic and disturbing."

D.J. gave him a look, and he could tell his cousin wasn't convinced that Ms. Edwards had been terrorized.

Sione sighed. "So what happened after we left the condo?"

"I took care of the situation."

"How did you take care of it?" Sione asked. "Did you call the cops?"

"I did," D.J. said. "The San Pedro police department plans to investigate."

"Do I have to make a statement?"

"Don't worry about that," D.J. said. "The cops don't know you were there and what do you really know about the situation? Nothing that could help their investigation."

"And what about Ms. Edwards?"

"The cops don't know she was there either," D.J. said. "I wanted the police to interrogate the hell out of her, but I figured she would bring your name into this mess, and you don't need to be associated, in any way, even indirectly, with some murder investigation."

"What makes you think somebody is dead?" Sione stared at D.J. "Just because a hand was cut off doesn't mean anybody was killed."

"I'm pretty sure that hand was chopped off a dead body," D.J. said.

Sione was sure of it too, but he didn't say anything. He couldn't. Not until he was absolutely sure of his suspicions about the severed hand.

"And I'm sure the hand was from a female," D.J. said. "I took a closer look at the hand before I called the cops. Soft skin, thin fingers. Nails painted. Which doesn't necessarily denote femininity, but I think the hand was chopped off a woman's wrist."

"And you think that woman was Maxine Porter?"

"Ms. Edwards thought so too," D.J. reminded him. "Don't you wonder how she's so sure that hand was chopped off Maxine's wrist and left on the floor?"

"I think she figured since it was Maxine's condo, then Maxine must have been killed," Sione said. "I don't think Spencer killed Maxine Porter."

"I actually don't either," D.J. confessed. "But she might have had something to do with her death. Or maybe she knows who chopped Maxine's hand off."

Sione shook his head. "Don't think so."

"Well, anyway," D.J. started. "So, when I was taking care of the situation, I searched Maxine Porter's condo and found a few interesting items. A burner phone, which I left for the cops to find. But I copied all the numbers from the phone log so I can check them out later. There was one number I deleted because I recognized it. That number was to your resort. Maxine Porter made several calls from that burner phone to the Belizean Banyan."

"And?"

"And I don't think she was calling to reserve a room," D.J. said. "She was calling Ms. Edwards."

"Well, that backs up Ms. Edwards' story," Sione said. "She said Maxine Porter called to tell her she'd found her driver's license at the boutique."

"I don't think their conversation was about the driver's license."

"Why do you say that?"

"Because when I searched Maxine Porter's condo, there was something else I found," D.J. said. "The box of Xanax."

47

San Ignacio, Belize
Belizean Banyan Resort - Honeymoon Casita

Spencer pressed two fingers into the center of her forehead as she paced from the foot of the bed to the mahogany wardrobe and back again.

The last three hours of her life had been spent updating her sisters about everything that had happened in San Pedro yesterday. Spencer had begun with the early morning call from Maxine Porter, demanding to see her because of some supposed problem with the medicine delivery. Then she'd told them about finding the severed hand on the floor in Maxine's closet right before that bastard Tommy Fong attacked her. Again.

She'd wrapped up her bizarre tale of horror and confusion with the most puzzling aspect of the story, recounting how John had shown up to rescue her from Fong. Saving the worst for last, Spencer had divulged about the photos John had secretly taken of her.

They'd discussed everything, in painstaking detail, and had speculated and deduced and extrapolated the hell out of the situation from every conceivable angle, even those which made no sense. Then they'd discussed everything again, coming to basically the same conclusion. Spencer had to get the favor done for Ben.

If she wanted to return to Texas without the fear of spending the best years of her life in an orange jumpsuit, then she had to find the envelope, or she would never get her hands on the video evidence Ben was blackmailing her with.

Dropping onto the settee at the foot of the bed, Spencer rubbed away the tears she'd tried not to shed since finding evidence of John's suspicions in that damn blue folder. Along with heart-stopping panic, a host of other dizzying emotions had besieged Spencer when she'd opened the file. Fear. Disappointment. Apprehension. Even anger and outrage.

Torn between confronting John for pretty much stalking her and fleeing the casita, Spencer chose the latter. Without bothering to say goodbye, she'd hastily donned her clothes, grabbed her purse from the guest bedroom, and slipped out of the casita.

Sprinting down the gravel path, Spencer had charged into the honeymoon casita and slammed the door behind her. She'd scanned the living room, trying to catch her breath, remembering John's fear about Tommy Fong returning to attack her again. His apprehension had been intense, prompting him to insist she stay with him last night—in his bed.

Lying next to John had felt perfect, as though she belonged in his arms. Cuddled next to him, she felt as though she was in a dream. A dream she'd been too afraid to indulge in, because she knew it would never come true for her. And it hadn't. What she'd thought was a dream had really been a nightmare.

John hadn't wanted her close to him because he might actually be interested in her. He didn't trust her. He'd pulled her into his arms because it was easier to watch her if she was only inches away from him. And now, despite everything that had happened to her, what scared her the most was realizing how disappointed she was that John wasn't interested.

She'd been so stupid, thinking the resort owner could possibly want someone like her, a woman he obviously believed was involved in something criminal. When she thought about the horrible childhood memory she'd shared with him, she cringed. Why the hell had she told him about something that still made her feel depressed and abandoned?

The destruction of her favorite doll, one of the few toys she had, for reasons she still didn't understand, was something even her sisters didn't know. And yet, she'd told John. Why? She wasn't sure. Maybe because she'd felt so comfortable in his arms, it was easy to be uninhibited.

"I know this might sound crazy," Rae said. "But maybe you should call Ben's bluff."

"Call his bluff? Are you serious?"

Shady said, "That sounds absolutely crazy."

"Hear me out," Rae said. "As crazy as it sounds, I think you should tell Ben to call the police and give them the evidence he's got on you."

"Well, I might as well just turn myself in," Spencer said. "If I do that, then I'm definitely going to jail!"

"Not necessarily," Rae said. "I really think you'd have a better chance with the Texas criminal justice system than with Ben Chang."

"And why the hell do you think that?"

Rae said, "I was talking to Mr. Cephas about it—"

"Why were you talking to him about me?"

"Mr. Cephas asked about you, and I told him about the crack you got your ass in."

"Wait, what?" Spencer was confused. "You told Mr. Cephas? Why would you do that?"

"Because I'm worried about you and I don't trust Ben Chang. If you think these side ventures and favors are going to stop once you find the envelope, then you're crazy."

"Ben promised me that he would give me the video and that he didn't make any more copies."

"Somebody call Lady Elaine Fairchild because this bitch is living in the land of make believe!"

"Desarae," Shady warned.

Spencer walked toward the French doors. "You can think I'm crazy, but I have to believe Ben is telling me the truth."

"Look, Mr. Cephas can get you a good lawyer," Rae said. "He's got a guy in mind. And this guy gets drug smugglers off, okay? Mr. Cephas is sure the guy can get the evidence against you thrown out as inadmissible. Or, if not, this lawyer will get you probation. Either way, you ain't going to jail."

"I don't know," Spencer said. "I think hoping and praying some lawyer will be able to get my case thrown out is too risky. I have to take my chances and believe that Ben will keep his word to me."

"Okay, then," Rae said. "If you insist on hoping and praying that Ben is gonna keep his word, then you need some insurance. Because I can guarantee you, he's lying to you."

"Insurance?" Shady asked.

"Spencer needs protection," Rae said. "Just in case Ben decides to come back asking for more favors, which he's gonna be able to do because, well whatdaya know, he has another copy of that video."

"What kind of insurance?" Spencer asked.

"You know that envelope Ben wants so bad," Rae said. "When you find it, you need to open it, and whatever is inside, you need to make a few copies of your own."

"Yeah, that's a great idea," Spencer said. "But what if I don't find the damn envelope."

"You will find it," Shady said.

"You don't know that, Shady," Spencer said. "And now that I know John is suspicious of me, I might never get another chance to get inside of his casita to look for the damn envelope!"

"Well, if you don't," Rae said. "It's your own damn fault."

Pissed, Spencer stared at her reflection in the glass panes of the French doors. "Excuse me?"

"After all that crazy shit went down in San Pedro," Rae said. "Sione damn near forced you to stay with him. Ben had told you to get a dinner date with Sione, and you told us that Sione offered to make you dinner yesterday. That was the perfect opportunity to slip a little GHB in his wine and—"

"I'm not using that damn GHB!" Spencer said. "Drugging men is the reason I'm in this mess right now!"

"No, you're in this mess because you didn't use the GHB!" Rae hollered back at her. "If you had drugged Ben, then he wouldn't have caught you—"

"No, if Spencer had drugged Ben, then he would have been passed out when Tommy Fong broke into the townhouse," Shady said. "And Tommy Fong might have hurt Spencer!"

"Are the two of you forgetting the damn interior surveillance in Ben's closet?" Spencer asked. "Even if I had drugged Ben and even if Tommy Fong hadn't broken into the townhouse, the fact remains that Ben would still have a video of me taking money and watches from his closet!"

"You know what," Rae said. "You're really in this mess because you "dated" Ben when you know you really didn't want to. You "dated" him because you didn't want to deal with your feelings for him."

Incensed and insulted, Spencer jumped up. "I'm in this mess because I let you talk me into "dating" in the first damn place!" Spencer hissed. "I'm in this mess because I was stupid enough to believe I could get away with stealing! I should have listened to Shady!"

Tense silence ensued. Spencer could hear the anger and frustration in the words her sisters weren't saying, the words they couldn't speak. Always one to avoid awkward confrontations, Shady was probably cringing and praying for a response to soothe the hurt feelings. Beyond livid, Rae was most likely taking a moment to catch her breath before she said something she might regret.

"I have to go," Spencer snapped and then tossed the cell phone onto the coffee table. Lightheaded, she stumbled to the couch and plopped down onto the cushions, pissed that the conversation with her sisters had turned venomous and accusatory.

Spencer sighed, wiping tears from her cheeks. She shouldn't have been so hateful and spiteful. The choice she'd made to start "dating" had been hers alone. She shouldn't have insinuated that she'd been tricked, or forced, into drugging men. She was a grown-ass woman, responsible for her own actions, good or bad. She'd have to call her sisters back and apologize. And she had to start with Rae, who needed to know that Spencer didn't really think she'd been coerced into "dating."

The cell phone rang. Her stomach jerked as she reached for it and decided she would answer with the apology she knew her sisters deserved. When she checked the caller ID, her heart sank a bit. It was her cousin Rusty, who she was usually happy to talk to, but she was anxious to make things right with her sisters. Still, Spencer answered the call.

"Spencer? Girl, where are you?" Rusty asked. "I've been calling and calling. Your phone keeps going to voice mail."

"Really?" Spencer said, realizing she probably hadn't been diligent about keeping her cell phone charged or about checking the messages. "Um, I'm in Belize."

"Belize?" Rusty sounded surprised. "What are you doing in Belize?"

"Vacation," Spencer lied. "What's going on?"

"First of all, don't panic because nobody is dead, hurt, or in the hospital."

"Okay, what happened?" Spencer asked, her pulse racing. "Was it something bad?

"Nana's house was broken into last night."

"Oh my God! Is she okay?"

"Yeah, she's fine," Rusty said. "She wasn't even there when it happened. She was at Bible study."

"Oh, thank God," Spencer said, breathing a bit easier.

"Girl, you know she's not afraid of anything," Rusty said. "She said she hopes the cops find them so she can pray for them. She told me they just need Jesus, that's all."

That didn't surprise Spencer. Her grandmother was very faithful and believed God's mercy and forgiveness was for everyone.

"The cops think it was some kids who thought it might be fun to vandalize a house."

"Stupid little assholes," Spencer said, shaking her head.

"Anyway, I was calling because me and Jennifer are going over there this weekend to help clean everything up, and I wanted to see if you could come help us," Rusty said. "But I didn't know you were on vacay."

"I wish I was in town so I could help y'all."

"Me too. Girl, they tore the damn house up," Rusty said. "Didn't take nothing, just broke a lot of dishes and lamps and vases. Anything made of glass, they smashed it. And they wrote a bunch of crazy shit all over the walls. Something like, the dragon will get you with fire, or some crap, I can't remember, but—"

Spencer was no longer listening. Trembling, she jumped up. Her cousin's words echoed in her head as the drawing on Ben's bedroom ceiling flashed before her eyes.

The tiger will strike with claws ... but the dragon will consume with fire.

"Hey, Rusty, I need to call you back."

48

"You sonofabitch!" Spencer screamed into the burner phone when Ben answered. "You had someone break into my grandmother's house!"

"Relax, sweet girl, she wasn't hurt."

"How could you do that!" she yelled, stomping across the master suite, pacing back and forth. "Why would you do that! She is an old woman who lives alone—"

"She wasn't even at home. I never planned for her to be there when the vandals broke in. She was at church, hopefully praying for her wayward, wicked granddaughter, who seems to think she can escape the consequences of her mistakes."

Dizzy from frustration and rage, Spencer sank back down on the edge of the bed. "I am not trying to escape the consequences for my mistakes!"

"Then why don't I have that envelope?"

Spencer took a deep breath. "I am still looking for it."

"No, you're playing house with Sione Tuiali'i and giving me excuses, telling me what you won't do."

"I will find the envelope," she said, clutching the burner phone so tight, she thought she might crack it.

"Have you searched the entire casita?"

"Not yet, but—"

"Did you use the GHB?"

"I told you, I'm not going to—"

"You are going to do exactly what I tell you," he said. "Go back to his casita. Use the GHB. Once Sione Tuiali'i is unconscious, you need to search every inch of his casita. Do not stop until you find that damn envelope."

"What if the envelope is not in his casita?"

"It has to be there," Ben said, after a slight hesitation, one she almost didn't catch. "The envelope is in that casita. Find it. Don't disappoint me. You have until the end of the week."

"The end of the week?" Panicked, Spencer stood again. "Today is Friday!"

"Then maybe you should hurry up and start looking."

"I can't guarantee that I'll find it in two days!" she said. "You have to give me more time!"

"Well, sweet girl, let me tell you what I can't guarantee," he said. "I can't guarantee that I won't burn your grandmother's house to the ground, and I can't guarantee that she won't be at home when I strike the match."

His threat hit her like a sledgehammer and took all the breath from her body, leaving her trembling and gasping. "No ..." She dropped to the floor, struggling to speak. "Please ... don't ... hurt—"

The cell phone slipped from Spencer's hand, banged against the hardwood floor, and skittered toward the settee at the foot of the bed. A hot mass formed in her throat, and as she struggled to swallow it, Spencer stared at the phone until it started to blur. A tear slid down her cheek and then another, salty trickles dripping from her chin.

––––––––

Will Spencer get the envelope in time? Or will she suffer a terrible fate at the hands of Ben? Find out in the next book in the Spencer and Sione Series, Her Deadly Threat.

Start reading today!

ALSO BY RACHEL WOODS

REPORTER ROLAND BEAN COZY MYSTERIES

Roland "Beanie" Bean, husband and loving father, finds himself the unwitting participant in solving crimes as he seeks to make a name for himself as a reporter for the *Palmchat Gazette*.

HAPPY BIRTHDAY MURDER

EASTER EGG HUNT MURDER

MERRY CHRISTMAS MURDER

TRICK OR TREAT MURDER

GOBBLE GOBBLE MURDER

HAPPY 4TH OF JULY MURDER

PALMCHAT ISLANDS MYSTERIES

Married journalists, Vivian and Leo, manage the island newspaper while solving crimes as they chase leads for their next story.

UNTIL DEATH DO US PART

NO ONE WILL FIND YOU

YOU WILL DIE FOR THIS

DON'T MAKE ME HURT YOU

THE PALMCHAT ISLANDS MYSTERIES BOX SET: BOOKS 1 - 4

SPENCER & SIONE SERIES

Gripping romantic suspense series with steamy romance, unpredictable plot twists and devastating consequences of deceit.

HER DEADLY MISTAKE

HER DEADLY DECEPTION

HER DEADLY THREAT

HER DEADLY BETRAYAL

MURDER IN PARADISE SERIES

A series of stand-alone women sleuth mysteries with murder, mayhem and a dash of romance, set against the backdrop of turquoise waters and swaying palm trees of the fictional Palmchat Islands.

THE UNWORTHY WIFE

THE PERFECT LIAR

THE SILENT ENEMY

ABOUT THE AUTHOR

Rachel Woods studied journalism and graduated from the University of Houston where she published articles in the Daily Cougar. She is a legal assistant by day and a freelance writer and blogger with a penchant for melodrama by night. Many of her stories take place on the islands, which she has visited around the world. Rachel resides in Houston, Texas with her three sock monkeys.

For more information:
www.therachelwoods.com
rachel@therachelwoods.com

facebook.com/therachelwoodsauthor

instagram.com/therachelwoodsauthor

bookbub.com/authors/rachel-woods

amazon.com/author/therachelwoods

ABOUT THE PUBLISHER

BonzaiMoon Books is a family-run, artisanal publishing company created in the summer of 2014. We publish works of fiction in various genres. Our passion and focus is working with authors who write the books you want to read, and giving those authors the opportunity to have more direct input in the publishing of their work.

For more information:
www.bonzaimoonbooks.com
info@bonzaimoonbooks.com

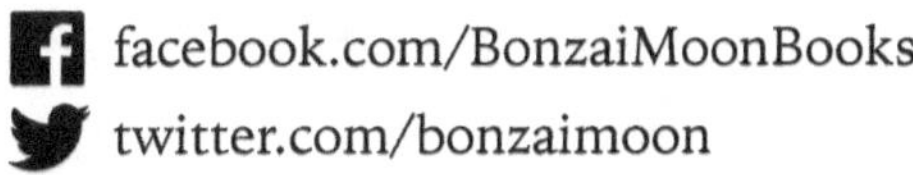